WISHES FOR BEGINNERS

Also by Eileen Cook

Fourth Grade Fairy

Fourth Grade Fairy

WISHES FOR BEGINNERS

Eileen Cook

Aladdin

New York London Toronto Sydney

This book is a work of fiction. Any references to historical events, real people, or real locales are used fictitiously. Other names, characters, places, and incidents are the product of the author's imagination, and any resemblance to actual events or locales or persons, living or dead, is entirely coincidental.

ALADDIN

An imprint of Simon & Schuster Children's Publishing Division
1230 Avenue of the Americas, New York, NY 10020
First Aladdin paperback edition June 2011
Copyright © 2011 by Eileen Cook
All rights reserved, including the right of reproduction in whole or in part in any form.
ALADDIN is a trademark of Simon & Schuster, Inc., and related logo is a registered trademark of Simon & Schuster, Inc.
For information about special discounts for bulk purchases, please contact Simon & Schuster Special Sales at 1-866-506-1949 or business@simonandschuster.com.
The Simon & Schuster Speakers Bureau can bring authors to your live event. For more information or to book an event contact the Simon & Schuster Speakers Bureau at 1-866-248-3049 or visit our website at www.simonspeakers.com.
Designed by Jessica Handelman and Karina Granda
The text of this book was set in Lomba.
Manufactured in the United States of America 0511 OFF
2 4 6 8 10 9 7 5 3 1
Library of Congress Control Number 2010932344
ISBN 978-1-4169-9812-9
ISBN 978-1-4169-9815-0 (eBook)

*To Mom and Dad, who taught me to
love books and always believed in the
power of imagination.*

one

The most exciting thing that could ever happen to my fourth-grade class would be:

    a. aliens from outer space come to suck us all up in their spaceship and take us to their planet where they make us their rulers.

    b. TV producers want to make a show about our class and we're all going to become famous. We'll wear giant sunglasses and carry our dogs around in handbags and everyone will want our autographs.

    c. the president has selected our class to be his official kid advisors. We'll have fancy dinners at the White House while he asks us what we think needs to happen in the world. Personally, I plan to make sure he saves the polar bear.

    d. none of the above.

★　★　★

I knew something really exciting *must* have happened because there was a big circle of people on the playground. Someone squealed and a couple of the girls were jumping up and down. They were bouncing all around like popcorn.

I saw my best friend Katie Hillegonds sitting on top of the slide. She liked to sit up there where she could see everything. I ran over to her. "What's going on?"

"I got a new book." Katie held it out. "It's all about NASA. My mom said it was for older kids, but I told her if I'm going to be an astronaut I couldn't read little kid books. Did you know there's no sound in space?" She didn't wait for me to answer. "The book is good, but I think it would be better with more pictures." She flipped through the pages.

I didn't always understand humans, or, as we call them in the fairy community, humdrums. I come from a long line of fairy godmothers, but I always wanted to be just a plain humdrum. Or at least that was what I wanted until I learned how much fun being magical could be. After all if I wasn't magical I wouldn't be able to talk to my dog and have him talk back. Also if

I hadn't been magical I also wouldn't have been able to save my sister from being eaten by a lizard. It wasn't a large lizard or anything, my sister was really small at the time, sort of firefly-size. Even though it wasn't a giant, mutant lizard, the rescue plan still required me to be pretty clever. Not that I'm bragging or anything. I'd decided that I would stick with being magical and have a humdrum as a friend instead.

Until this school year I'd always attended the Cottingley Fairy Academy across town. I'd convinced my parents to let me study humdrums up close as long as no one figured out that I was a fairy. I'd only been going to Riverside Elementary for a couple of months. There were still a lot of things I didn't understand, but I was sure about this. No one in our class was excited that Katie had a book about rockets.

"Neat. It looks like a cool book." One tip for getting along with humdrums is that you should always act interested in things they're interested in, even if you aren't. For example, if your best friend has a pet bird you should pretend that you find it really fascinating that they clean themselves by having dust baths. (Even though taking a dust bath sounds like a stupid way to get clean.) "So, do you know why everyone else is so excited?" I asked trying to pull Katie's attention back.

Katie looked down at the cluster of girls. "Oh. Miranda's going to be in a wedding."

I watched Miranda's friend Bethany act like she was going to faint because she was so thrilled. Bethany has always been a drama queen, but even the other girls seemed excited. "Is it that big of a deal?"

Katie closed her book with a snap. "Exactly! Who cares that she gets to be a bridesmaid? If you ask me, a bunch of wedding cake doesn't make up for having to wear a fancy dress that itches and uncomfortable shoes."

My forehead wrinkled while I thought about it. I could think of a lot of things that sounded more fun than wearing uncomfortable shoes. However, my mom granted more wedding wishes than any other. Fairy godmothers spent a lot of time on romance, so there must be something to it.

"My dress is going to be light pink, and we're going to carry bouquets of pink and white roses," I overheard Miranda say. The cluster of girls all sighed together.

"Roses mean true love," Bethany said. "Every flower has a meaning, you know." A few of the girls nodded. Bethany always had to be an expert on everything. "You have to be really careful about what you put in a wedding bouquet or you could doom the entire marriage."

I wasn't sure about the meaning of roses, but I was pretty sure Bethany was wrong about the part about the wrong flowers ruining things.

"I wonder what dandelions mean?" Paula asked.

Bethany ignored Paula.

"I'm not just some regular junior bridesmaid. I'm responsible for holding my cousin's bouquet during the wedding ceremony so she can concentrate on getting married." Miranda shrugged. "It's a pretty important job."

Everyone was silent for a moment as if they were awed by what Miranda would have to do. They were acting like she would be diffusing a bomb instead of holding a bunch of flowers. Humdrums were very confusing sometimes.

The bell rang. Katie jumped up and surfed down the slide with her arms out to keep her balance. I went down the ladder. If I tried to go down standing, I would fall for sure, and if I sat down to slide, Bethany would make fun of me for acting like a kid. Fourth grade is really complicated. Sometimes it's okay to be a kid and other times everyone acts grown up. The hard part is figuring out which time you're supposed to act which way. It would be a lot easier if there were a rule book. And so part of my deal with my parents to attend humdrum school was that I had agreed to do presentations about humdrums to other sprites at the fairy academy. How was I supposed to help future fairy godmothers understand humdrums when I couldn't make sense of what they did half the time?

"I think it's cool you're going to be a junior bridesmaid," I said to Miranda as we lined up to go inside. "I'd love to see your dress sometime." Katie was my best friend, but I still couldn't help being fascinated by Miranda. It wasn't just me. Everyone in our entire school liked Miranda, including the really cranky lunch lady who would give her extra applesauce. Even the fifth graders liked Miranda and they spent most of their time ignoring the rest of us. I couldn't help thinking it would be really cool to have Miranda as a friend, too.

"Do you think she's going to wear her bridesmaid dress to school?" Bethany asked. "Duh, Willow." She rolled her eyes at Paula.

I ignored Bethany. "Maybe you could bring in a picture of it."

"I should bring the picture of my cousin's dress. It is

the most beautiful dress you've ever seen. It was on the cover of *Brides* magazine. It's strapless and the skirt has layers of lace and sort of swooshes down with all these beads and sequins on it."

All the girls around us gave another sigh of pleasure. I pulled my small humdrum notebook out of my bag and scribbled in it. *Dresses are better the more sparkle they have.* You never knew how humdrum information could be useful. Someday I might have to grant a dress wish and now I would know to add a bit of extra glitter.

Nathan, who was behind Miranda in line, snatched the notebook out of my hand and held it above his head. This wouldn't be a big deal except for the fact that he was the tallest person in our class. "Got your diary!" He yelled out.

"Give it back." I jumped up, trying to take it back from him, but I couldn't reach. He moved in a circle laughing.

"Who wants to hear Willow's secrets?" His friends laughed, which just encouraged him. "Dresses are better with more sparkle," he read out. "Aw, are you dreaming about your own wedding?"

My face was red hot. What if he flipped the pages

and read the other things in there? I was pretty sure no one else in my class had to take notes on how to fit in. I jumped up, but unless I could fly like my sister, this was never going to work. "Please give it to me," I begged him. I looked around, hoping that our teacher, Ms. Caul, would come out and make him hand it over, but she was still inside. There's never a grown-up around when you want one.

Nathan cocked his head to the side. "Willow wants a wedding of her very own. Isn't that romantic?" He fluttered his eyelashes and put a sappy smile on his face. "She's in looooooove."

"Who is she going to find to marry *her*?" Bethany asked, and Nathan laughed.

Nathan held my notebook in the hand above his head as he tried to flip the pages to read more. "Maybe she says in here who she loves."

"Give it back," Katie demanded. Nathan laughed. Katie was even shorter than me. There was no way she was going to be able to grab the notebook. Unless there was a miracle, my life was about to be ruined. Nathan would read out all of my notes and everyone would make fun of me for the rest of the year. If my dog Winston was around I would make him run over and chew Nathan's lips off. He wouldn't do so much talking if he didn't have any lips.

Katie jabbed Nathan hard in the stomach. He gave a loud *oomph* and bent over. Katie grabbed the notebook out of his hand and gave it back to me.

"Hey, you aren't supposed to hit people," Bethany yelled out.

"Hey, you aren't supposed to steal things," Katie said with her hand on her hip, copying Bethany.

I clutched the notebook to my chest. I was never going to let it out of my hands again. I might ask my mom to enchant it so that if any humdrums ever got a hold of it again, all it would show was pages with nothing on them other than *Nathan Filler is a big jerk.*

Ms. Caul came out and clapped her hands. "Okay, everyone, we're supposed to be in a line."

I held my breath to see if Bethany would tell on Katie. Ms. Caul might want to look at my notebook to see what all the trouble was about. Even though I thought she was the best teacher in the whole world—and smelled like vanilla—I didn't want her to read it either. No one said anything; they shuffled back into a line so we could follow Ms. Caul into school.

"Willow is in wuuuve," Nathan whispered, making

his voice sound like little kid. The entire line of fourth graders snickered.

I spun around and glared at him. He put his hand under his shirt and made his shirt pump in and out as if his heart was beating like crazy.

That was it. Nathan Filler was going to have to pay.

two

The brown gloppy stuff they serve for hot lunch:

a. smells like what would happen if you set garbage on fire.

b. tastes like it was made out of monkey fur, glue, and fish guts.

c. provides the perfect way for me to get revenge.

d. all of the above. (Although I didn't actually taste it, I'm guessing what it tasted like based on how it looked and smelled.)

I only had hot lunch on the days when they had cheese pizza. The other days my mom packed my lunch.

"Are those carrots?" Katie asked.

My mom had used magic to make my carrots into the shape of penguins. She liked to make my lunch interesting. She didn't seem to understand that the humdrum idea of an interesting lunch was to cut peanut butter sandwiches on the diagonal instead of down the middle. "Um. My mom likes to carve stuff," I mumbled.

Katie took one out of my hand and looked it over, her eyes wide. "This is so cool. You can see where it has individual feathers. You don't see these every day."

I took it back and bit into it. "My mom's really into crafts." I peeked in my bag and realized my mom had toasted the bread on my sandwich in a complicated checkerboard pattern. I quickly tore it into pieces so that the pattern wasn't obvious.

"Maybe some time I could come over after school and your mom can show me how to make my carrots like that."

"I don't know." I stalled. "I think it would be more fun to go to your place. We could make a new book about Crackers in space. He'd look pretty funny in a helmet." Katie liked to write her own books, and then we would draw the pictures for them. She was going to have a whole library of them someday. Katie wanted to be an author. And an astronaut. And a famous soccer player. Katie was going to be a very busy grown-up.

"We never go to your house," Katie said.

"My sister is always there. She'd yell at us to be quiet so she could work on her homework." This was true. My older sister, Lucinda, was a know-it-all. She never let me play with her stuff, and she was always bragging about how she could fly. Although my sister was a pain, she wasn't the real reason I never invited Katie over. I didn't invite her over because I knew there was nothing about our house that was normal. Katie would figure out there was something funny about our family for sure. Even more funny than penguin-shaped carrots.

A French fry plopped down on our table making both Katie and me jump. I spun around. Nathan threw another fry, and it hit me in the center of my forehead.

"Here's a snack for your wedding buffet," Nathan said, and everyone at his table laughed.

"He's lucky that fry didn't have ketchup on it," Katie said.

"Why is he being so mean?" I asked.

Katie shrugged. "Who knows? He's a boy."

Nathan was one of the most popular boys in our class. He was really good at sports. In gym he was always picked first for everything. This could explain why he was so good at throwing fries. He had blond hair that sort of flopped over one eye. He was cute, but he knew it.

I knew I wasn't supposed to do any magic at school, but he threw a fry at me. People should never throw vegetables at another person. That should be a rule. I called out to Theodore.

Theodore was the mouse that lived in the walls of the school cafeteria. I don't want to brag or anything, but my magical ability as a fairy is that I can talk to animals. This is pretty special. I don't know any other fairies who can do this. It's a pretty handy skill. For example, my dog Winston can tell me exactly what he wants for dinner. It's almost never kibble. He'd rather have pork chops.

Theodore stuck his pink nose out of the tiny hole in the wall. His whiskers flicked back and forth. He was pretty chunky, so his behind was still stuck in the wall. He lived off the scraps from the cafeteria, and there are a lot of leftovers in a school cafeteria. I quickly explained to him what Nathan had done.

"How dare he throw food! Gentlemen should never accost a lady." Theodore shook his head as if he couldn't believe what he heard. He was a very old-fashioned type of mouse. "That boy needs to be taught a lesson. Stand aside, fair maiden, and allow me to teach this rogue proper manners."

Theodore grunted and his bottom popped out of the hole like a cork coming out of a bottle. He waddled along the wall until he was in the middle of the cafeteria. He took several deep breaths to ready himself for the challenge.

"Revenge!" Theodore yelled as he ran full speed toward Nathan's table. No one saw him until he ran up the table leg. Then one of the fifth-grade girls spotted him and began to scream.

Theodore shoved all the lunch trays on the table, grunting with the effort. The trays slid along the slick tabletop and fell straight into Nathan's lap. The beef stew splashed down, covering him in thick brown goo. His mouth was open in shock. I couldn't tell if that was from the hot stew soaking through his shirt and pants or the fact that a mouse was the one that dumped the food on him.

"Now let that be a lesson to you," Theodore said, brushing his front paws off before he jumped down. "A gentleman conducts himself with honor and treats women with respect."

The fifth-grade girls were all standing on their chairs screaming and pointing. "Easy ladies, no need to get all riled up. I only use my might on those that deserve it." Theodore headed back toward his hole, the kids parting to make a path for him. One of the lunch ladies came skidding out of the kitchen with giant metal cookie tray over her head. When Theodore saw her, he took off running. He hit the hole at full speed. He was stuck for a second. I held my breath, terrified the lunch lady would catch up with him and whack him with the tray, but his back legs kept pushing and he popped back in the hole.

Bethany rushed over to Nathan with a stack of napkins. "Are you okay?"

"Did you see that?" Nathan stammered. "That mouse attacked me. It was like it was rabid or something. He stared right at me, and I swear he looked mad."

I coughed to cover up the fact that I wanted to laugh. There were gravy-covered noodles in his shirt pocket. He even had some peas in his hair. When I turned back around Katie was staring at me with one eyebrow raised.

"Wow. That sure was weird, huh?" I asked, shoving

a carrot in my mouth. I didn't meet her eyes in case she could tell I was somehow involved.

"Yeah. Sure was weird. I guess it was another one of those things that you just don't see every day."

three

True or False:

When you are in trouble, even cookies won't taste as good as they normally do.

Answer:

True. However, they still taste pretty good and definitely better than Brussels sprouts, which taste like mildewed washcloths.

Nathan came back to class after lunch. He was stuck wearing clothes from the lost and found box, including a goofy looking pink sweatshirt with sleeves that were too short. His stew-covered things were in a plastic shopping bag. I bet they were going to smell nasty by the time he got home. That thought made me happy up until Nathan passed Ms. Caul a note. I should have known I'd get caught. Having a mouse go all crazy in the cafeteria wasn't exactly subtle.

She read the note quickly and then looked up. "Willow? You're needed in the principal's office."

I pointed silently to my chest just in case there was another Willow she wanted. Ms. Caul nodded, and I felt my stomach fall to the floor. Uh-oh.

"But we're in the middle of math," I said, holding up my worksheet. I tried to make my face look really serious. I shouldn't miss a lesson on fractions—they were pretty important. Maybe if Ms. Caul realized how interested I was in fractions she would let me stay. She was always saying how important it was to learn.

"That's all right. You can finish your sheet later."

I stood next to my desk waiting to see if I could think of another reason that I couldn't leave the room. I could feel everyone else staring at me. I sighed. I was doomed.

I walked down the hall to the office. I dragged my feet on the floor so that my tennis shoes made a squeaky sound, not walking more than one square tile at a time so I could delay getting to the office as long as possible. I don't think anyone wants to go to the principal's office, but it was extra bad for me because the principal was my grandma. When I got to her office the door opened before I even touched the plate that spelled out her name, Glinda Doyle.

"Why don't you come in and have a seat?" Grandma was sitting in her giant leather chair behind her desk. As I sat down, Grandma slid a china plate with cookies on it towards me. "Would you like an oatmeal cookie? They're from your mom's bakery."

I took a cookie and nibbled on the edges. There didn't seem to be a lot of room in my stomach because it was in a tight ball. Usually I could always fit in one of my mom's cookies. Humdrums and fairies both agreed that she ran the best bakery in town.

"I wondered if you could help me with something," Grandma asked. "Did you see what happened in the cafeteria today?"

My throat seized shut. The bite of cookie couldn't go the rest of the way down. "Um, sure."

"Do you know anything about it?" She looked at me over the top of the glasses perched on the very end of her nose.

I put the cookie down. I couldn't lie to my grandma. I felt my lower lip start to shake. I was absolutely for-bidden from doing magic at school. It was a rule. If

Grandma told my dad then he might make me leave and go back to Cottingley Fairy Academy. I wouldn't be able to see Katie anymore, and then she would find a new best friend at school.

"I didn't mean to do it! It was an accident," I wailed. The tears started to flow. "Nathan's been mean to me all day. He keeps teasing me, and he took my notebook. He wouldn't give it back. He was going to read it. He only gave it back because Katie hit him and then he threw food at me." I gave a big hiccup, but before I could explain any more, my grandma put her hand on top of mine.

"Take it easy. Let's start at the beginning. What's Nathan teasing you about?"

"About getting married. Not that I want to get married. I don't even like anyone, but everyone was talking about weddings and dresses. Then in my notebook I made this note about what people want for their wedding dresses in case I ever have to grant a wish, but he thought I was planning my own wedding."

Grandma sat back. "Let me guess, all of this started because Miranda gets to be a junior bridesmaid in her cousin's wedding."

"How did you know?"

"How do you think Miranda got picked to be in the wedding?" Grandma's eyes twinkled.

"You granted that wish?" I whistled. Grandma was good. No wonder she was a Fairy Godmother Level Three.

"Now why do you suppose Nathan is teasing you?" Grandma pushed the plate of cookies back toward me. Now that I'd told the truth my stomach was far less tense, and I was pretty sure I could fit a cookie in. Maybe even two cookies.

"I don't know. We used to get along. He picked me for his team in gym class once, and we were partners on the science museum field trip."

"I think I know why," Grandma said with a smile. "I think he likes you."

I wrinkled up my nose. I wasn't sure how I felt about that idea. "But if he likes me why would he tease me?"

"Sometimes humdrum boys do that. They don't know how to say they like you, so they tease you instead."

I scratched my nose while I thought about that. "Wouldn't it make more sense for them to send flowers? On humdrum TV shows they're always sending flowers or candy if they like someone. They don't throw French fries at them. Ever."

"Life isn't always like humdrum TV," Grandma took another cookie. "That's something else you might want to put in your notebook."

I pulled my notebook out and put in Grandma's advice along with a note about how humdrum boys throw things to show their affection. It's a wonder humdrums ever get married if the boys act so stupid. No wonder the girls were so excited about a wedding. Seeing a couple actually admit they like each other must be a pretty big deal. Plus there are sparkly dresses and cake. Fairies tend to be more practical: If you like someone you just tell them. Although, I've heard stories about boy fairies having unicorns deliver flowers to the girls they like. It's sort of splashy, but it still is pretty neat. Unless the unicorn eats your flowers.

"Now that we've sorted out what Nathan was up to, do you want to explain what you were thinking when you had that mouse dump food all over him?"

"That was Theodore's idea," I explained.

"But did you happen to talk to Theodore about the situation?"

I looked down at my lap. "Are you going to tell my dad that I broke the rules?"

"Let's say this time you bent the rules. I suppose we could keep this bent rule just between us."

My heart sped up. She wasn't going to tell my dad. Grandmas are the best. She leaned forward.

"However, I don't expect to see any more hocus-pocus in the hallways."

"Yes, ma'am." I nodded.

"Or in the classroom, the cafeteria, or on the playground. Now, there is a lot you can learn from this situation. I'm glad you're friends with Katie, but there are lots of other humdrums here, and you're going to have to learn how to get along with all of them."

"Even Bethany?" I asked.

She nodded. "Nathan, too." Grandma stood and came around the desk. "All right, give me a hug and then you better get back to math."

I threw my arms around her. "Thanks, Grandma. I really am sorry. I won't do it again. Going to school here is the best thing that ever happened to me."

"You're a special kid, Willow. Not just because you're my granddaughter." She held my chin in her hand and looked me in the eye. "You never know, you going to school here might be the best thing that happened to any of us."

four

True or False:

If you aren't sure what to do, getting your answers from a TV show is really bad idea.

Answer:

True. Unless you know the right shows to watch. Which I don't.

When I came home my mom was crying in front of our humdrum TV. This would worry me except for the fact that my mom did this almost every afternoon. She liked to watch what she called "soap operas," which didn't make much sense to me because they weren't about soap and no one was singing opera music. I also didn't understand why you would want to watch TV that made you want to cry, but grown-ups are weird.

Then I noticed there was a wedding happening on the TV. I plunked down on the sofa next to my mom. "Why are you crying? Aren't weddings supposed to be happy?"

"I'm crying because I'm happy. They've loved each other for a very long time, but they almost didn't end up together. The groom thought the bride had been killed in an accident, but she wasn't dead. She hit her head and lost her memory.

"The bride had an evil stepsister who had faked her own death because she was part of a terrorist plot. The evil sister always hated the bride and wanted her out of the picture. Once the bride was gone the evil stepsister pretended to come back from the dead because she wanted the bride's boyfriend for herself.

"The bride didn't know who she was," Mom went on. "She lived in this town far away, but she always knew something was missing. I mean other than her memory. She knew there was someone special out there for her. Despite the lies the stepsister was telling, the groom knew she was no good. When he refused to be with the evil sister, she sent a terrorist after him to rough him up. The bride was working in the hospital and the groom came in with a broken leg. As soon as she saw him she remembered everything and they fell into each other's arms. They decided to get married right there in the hospital right then so they would never be apart again." Mom sniffed. "It's so romantic."

"Wow." I watched the TV. I wondered where the bride had gotten such a sparkly wedding dress in the hospital. She must have a really good fairy godmother. The groom had a giant cast on his leg, but he was still moving pretty good. Romance seemed really complicated. "You grant a lot of wedding wishes, don't you, Mom?"

"Weddings are my specialty. I love everything about them. That's why I started the bakery. Weddings need cakes and wishes. This gives me a chance to accomplish both things at the same time."

"Why do you like to grant wishes for weddings? Is it the dresses?"

"I like the dresses. I think everyone should get to dress like a princess at least once."

"And, weddings have lots of flowers." I thought of the girls talking about the rose bouquet Miranda would carry. It had been pretty clear the flowers were a big deal.

"Yes, the flowers are nice too. Of course, weddings

aren't really about the dress, flowers, or the cake. Those things are nice, but that's not what's required to have a happy wedding. All you really need is true love."

I fidgeted on the sofa and then turned to face my mom. "Can I ask you something? A boy at school kept throwing French fries at me during lunch."

Mom smiled. "It sounds like he likes you."

I rolled my eyes. Apparently Mom knew all about the humdrum boy habit of throwing fried food at those they liked. It must be a long-standing tradition. "That's what Grandma said too. I figure if I liked him back I could toss some celery sticks at him to let him know, but what do I do if I don't like him?" I thought about Nathan's smile. He smiled sideways, like his mouth was crooked. It might be the kind of thing girls would think was cute if he wasn't a vegetable-throwing, notebook thief.

Mom tucked her bare feet under her giant skirt. "Hmm, that's a tricky one. It's important to be nice. You don't want to hurt his feelings."

I nodded. I hoped Grandma wouldn't tell her about how I arranged for stew to be dumped all over him. I would get a lecture on how Lucinda would never do something like that. My sister and I got along better ever since I saved her from being eaten by a lizard, but we still fought a lot. You would assume that after a life-saving rescue she would be forever grateful, but she was only sometimes grateful.

"I think the best thing you could do is tell this boy that you like him, but only as a friend," my mom suggested. "Find him on the playground and have a face-to-face chat."

Sometimes I wondered if parents were ever kids. Their advice always made me think they were born grown-ups. "I'll think about that idea," I said. When your parents come up with a totally crazy idea, you have to act like you are at least considering it. There was no way I was going to go up to Nathan and tell him I wanted to be friends.

When my mom got up to leave I stayed to watch the next show. It was about a woman who had a long-lost evil twin sister who was trying to break up her relation-ship. My dog Winston came downstairs yawning. He jumped up onto the sofa next to me and nudged my hand so I would rub his ears.

"Woo. Busy day," Winston said. "I'm beat."

I rolled my eyes. "You just got up from a nap. I can tell because the fur on your back is sticking up."

"Napping is a serious business. I have to fit in an

afternoon nap in between watching out for squirrels in the backyard, chewing on my fuzzy hot-dog toy, *and* guarding the house. I'm a very busy dog."

"Guarding the house?" I raised one eyebrow in disbelief.

"Do you see a bunch of burglars in here?" Winston asked giving his ears a quick scratch with his back paw. "No, you do not. Ergo, I've done my job. Now why are you so grumpy?"

"I have a problem with a boy at school."

"Do you want me to bite him?" Winston jumped up. "Or I could just scare him." Winston curled his lips back and growled.

"You would be scarier if your tail wasn't wagging." I pointed to his back end, which was whipping back and forth.

Winston turned around and looked disgustedly at his tail. "Darn tail. Can't control it. Gives me away every time."

"I need to come up with something to say to him that will make him be nice to me, but won't make him think I like him. It's hopeless." I sighed. The music on the TV show started up again. Suddenly I sat straight up. I had an idea. I should have known humdrum TV would have the answers!

five

Bad ideas happen because:

    a. they act like good ideas until you think more about it. (Bad ideas are really good at faking they are good ideas, otherwise no one would ever do them.)

    b. you've had too much ice cream and aren't thinking straight.

    c. the only advice you get on the idea comes from your dog, who is very cute, but not the best problem solver.

The note was a bit damp and crumply from being clutched in my pocket all morning. I wasn't so sure it was a good idea anymore. Maybe taking advice from a soap opera wasn't the best way to deal with this situation, after all my sister was sometimes evil to me, but she wasn't the type to get involved in terrorist plots. After dinner Winston and I had run up to my room to write a note to Nathan. The note explained that although I knew he liked me, it would never work out between the two of us. We had used some of the ideas from the soap operas we'd watched. Last night I thought it was brilliant, but now I was starting to rethink my plan.

What if my grandma and mom were wrong? My eyes slid over to look at Nathan. He had two milk straws stuffed under his upper lip and was pretending to be a walrus. He didn't seem to be paying any attention to me at all.

"Why do you keep staring at Nathan?" Katie asked. She took a loud sip from her juice box.

I spun back around to face her. "I wasn't staring at him." My face flushed bright red.

Katie's face scrunched up. "Is everything okay?"

"Why wouldn't everything be okay?" I said, my voice sounding screechy. I gave a fake laugh, but I could tell Katie knew I was only pretending. It wasn't a very good fake laugh. I sounded like what would happen if someone stepped on a goose.

Katie put her sandwich down. "If something's wrong, you can tell me. You can tell me anything."

"I know." I couldn't look her straight in the face. Best friends might tell each other everything, but I wasn't allowed to tell her I was a fairy. That counted as a pretty big secret. And because I couldn't tell her I was a fairy, I couldn't tell her about how I could understand my dog, Winston, or why my family was so weird or a million other things. There were more secrets I couldn't tell her than things I could tell her.

"Okay, if you weren't staring at Nathan, what were you looking at?"

"Um." My mind spun around trying to come up with a good answer. "I was looking to see how long the milk line is. I want a chocolate milk." I stood up. "Do you want one?"

Katie shook her head no. I walked slowly past Nathan's table in case he wanted to throw something at me, but he didn't. Not even a grape. If he was going to throw anything it would be grape, they were round and ball shaped. Throwing a grape doesn't take any effort at all, especially for someone who was as good at sports as he was. If Nathan had liked me it seemed like he didn't anymore. Not that I cared. It wasn't like I wanted someone with drinking-straw walrus tusks to be my boyfriend anyway.

I stood in the milk line and pulled out the note. I had written it with my sister's quill pen. It seemed like too important of a note to write in pencil, but the ink had gotten all over my hand like blue freckles. I looked down at the note with Nathan's name written on the outside in curly letters with TOP SECRET written in block letters on top. Thank goodness I hadn't given it to him yet. I tossed it into the trash can.

"What's this?" Bethany snatched the note out of the trash. She must have been standing right behind me.

"You can't have that," I said. Who takes things from the trash? The whole point of the trash is that it's garbage. I tried to grab the note from her, but Bethany yanked it away.

"Is this a love letter?" Bethany unfolded the note. She started to laugh when she read the first few lines. "Oh, Nathan! You have to hear this." Bethany's voice carried across the cafeteria. If my magic power were disappearing it wouldn't matter how much trouble I would be in, I would have disappeared right then. Just in case it might work I wished that the floor would open up and let me sink into the basement, but nothing happened.

I didn't need to hear Bethany read the note out loud. I knew exactly what it said.

> Dear Nathan,
>
> I know that you like me. There is no point in asking how I know, I just do. I am writing to tell you that it will never work out between us. It would be better if you liked someone else.
>
> My life is very complicated, and I am not always who I seem. I am dealing with an evil twin sister who has a plot to blow up the world. As a result I am in hiding here at school until I can find a way to rescue everyone. Maybe we will meet again years from now in another place.
>
> Willow

"I didn't know you had a twin sister," Paula said surprised.

Everyone in the cafeteria was laughing. The note sounded worse when it was read. I knew I should have left the piece about needing to save the world out, but that was Winston's favorite part of the soap opera we watched. He thought it made me sound very heroic and that Nathan would be let down easier if he thought I had to beat my evil twin sister. Now I could tell it sounded goofy. I turned and ran out of the cafeteria.

Katie found me in the library in the reading nook. She handed me the bag with the rest of my lunch in it. "You could have told me you liked Nathan," she said.

"I don't like him," I said. "He likes me. That's why I wrote the note. I wasn't sure how to get him to stop liking me."

"Well, I don't think you have to worry about that anymore." Katie sat down on the floor next to me.

"What did Nathan say?" I asked.

"Do you really want to know?" Katie asked. She waited for me to nod before saying anything. "He and his friends were calling you Super Willow, sort of like you were a super hero. 'Save the planet, Super Willow!' That kind of thing. Paula's still trying to figure out why she never knew about your sister."

I sighed. I couldn't even have Bethany attacked by a bunch of sea gulls because I had promised my grandma no more magic at school. "I'm never going to be able to face anyone in our class. I'm going to have to move to the middle of the desert to start all over again."

"You don't have to face anybody by yourself. We'll just tell people it was a joke. Besides if you move to the desert you'll get sand in everything you own. Who wants sand in their shorts?"

I felt myself starting to smile. Katie always cheered me up. "I suppose the desert is too hot to have ice cream too."

"And instead of your dog, you would have to have a camel, and I hear they really stink." Katie started to giggle.

"And I'd have a sunburn all the time," I said.

"And then your nose would peel." Katie pretended to peel giant sheets of skin off her nose.

"Okay, you've convinced me. I'll stay."

"Yay!" Katie threw her arm around me. "Here's the plan for when we get back to class. Ignore Bethany, she never has anything nice to say anyway. The whole reason she's being so snotty is because she likes Nathan."

"She does?" My mouth fell open. I had no idea.

"Yeah. She's totally boy crazy. She's always mooning over Nathan, trying to be his partner for school projects and stuff." Katie folded up her legs so she was sitting cross-legged. She was superflexible because she took gymnastics. Katie was involved in all sorts of activities after school.

"Why does Bethany love Nathan?" I asked.

Katie shrugged. "I think she loves being in love."

"I'm sorry I didn't talk to you about all of this." I stared down at my lap. I should have told her about Nathan, but I guess I was so used to keeping secrets I had forgotten to tell her the things I could. This humdrum thing was harder than it looked.

"It's okay." Katie crooked her pinky finger and I locked fingers with her. We shook on it. "No more secrets," Katie said.

I crossed my fingers behind my back so the lie wouldn't count. "No more secrets," I repeated.

six

In order to be a wedding expert, you should:
   a. have planned at least a hundred fancy weddings.
   b. have gone to college for a degree in party planning.
   c. at least been a guest at a couple of weddings.
   d. once helped your mom frost a wedding cake. (Although you accidentally stuck your elbow in the cake and made a small dent. Very small. It was filled in with frosting.)

My mom's bakery, Enchanted Sugar, was one of my favorite places in the whole world. The building looks like a giant frosted cake. It's bright white and all the fancy curlicue wood is painted pink. The wood floors are always shiny and there are four white metal tables with ice-cream parlor chairs so that if you can't wait to try your cupcake, then you can sit down and have one right then and there.

The front window always had a couple sample cakes so people could think about what they might want. Inside there was a big glass case full of cookies and cupcakes. Even though it looked really good, that was nothing compared to how it smelled! When you walked by you could smell pumpkin, cinnamon, caramel, vanilla, chocolate, and butterscotch. You could see people outside the window stop and sniff. Even if they planned to walk right past, they had to stop and try something.

Friday after school I was helping my mom. I don't want to brag or anything, but I'm a really good cupcake froster. The secret is in the wrist action, you have to give it a bit of a swirl at the end, and then top it with just a bit of sprinkles. You can't clump the sprinkles on. No one wants a clumpy cupcake.

I heard the bell above the door, and my mom greeted someone who was looking for a wedding cake. Brides from all over came to Enchanted Sugar for their wedding cakes. They thought they picked us because our cakes were tasty and beautiful. What they didn't know was that each cake came sprinkled with a bit of happily-ever-after magic. The magic was what made them really special.

"Can you make a cake with pink flowers on top?"

My head snapped up. I knew that voice. It was Miranda from school. I hurried to put all the cupcakes I was working on onto a silver tray. Then I took a finger full of frosting and smeared it on my cheek. I wanted to look like I was working superhard. I carried the cupcakes out to the front of the store.

"Willow?" Miranda was with her cousin, the future bride. I tried to act like I was surprised to see her. I put down my cupcakes and smiled.

"Is this one of your friends from school?" Mom asked. "Why don't you give her a cupcake, and we'll be right back." Mom led the bride-to-be toward the back where she kept a photo album full of the different styles of cakes.

"This is your mom's bakery?" Miranda sounded impressed, which just goes to show what good taste she has (with the exception of picking Bethany as a best friend).

"Uh-huh." I handed her one of the red-velvet cupcakes with cream-cheese icing. They were my favorite. I put the rest of the cupcakes on the stand in the display case. I made a big deal of making sure they were arranged perfectly. I would put one down, back up so I could see how it looked, and then move it just a smidge.

"You work here too?" Miranda asked, looking around with her eyes wide. I could understand her being impressed. Most likely I was the only fourth grader with a job.

"Of course." I wiped my hands on my lime green daisy apron. "I was going to tell you at school that if you have any questions about being a junior bridesmaid you should feel free to ask me. I've helped with a lot of weddings, so I'm sort of an expert." I shrugged like it wasn't a big deal.

When I said "a lot of weddings" that might have been stretching the truth. I had helped my mom with a wedding cake once, and over the past couple days I'd been reading all sorts of stuff about humdrum weddings. I'd even found a humdrum TV show all about choosing wedding dresses. I bet if you added up all the time I'd spent lately thinking about weddings, it would be almost a college degree's worth.

"Wow." Miranda was looking at me with wide eyes.

"As a bridesmaid you should make sure you have Band-Aids and some safety pins with you." I had gotten this advice from one of the TV shows I'd seen. "You never know when the bride might get a blister or a small tear in her dress, and then you're ready to help."

Miranda nodded. "That's a good idea."

"Like I said, I've helped with lots of these."

"What kind of earrings do you think bridesmaids should wear?" Miranda leaned on the counter. "My mom thinks I should wear a small pearl stud."

I shook my head. "Well, it depends on the dress, but I think something sparkly would be better. It's hard to say without seeing the dress."

"Do you want to come over and see it?"

I wanted to dance behind the counter. Miranda, the most popular girl in the entire fourth grade (so popular that the fifth-grade girls talked to her), had invited me to her house!

"I'm having a slumber party tomorrow night. You should come," Miranda said.

"Who else is going?"

"Bethany and Paula. We're going to watch movies, and my mom says we can stay up as late as we want. I have all my cousin's old bridal magazines. We're going to pick out what we would wear if it were our wedding. You can help since you're an expert."

I wasn't crazy about spending the night with Bethany,

but since it was the first time Miranda had asked me over I didn't think I could tell her who else to invite. "Okay, I'll ask my mom."

My mom and the bride-to-be came out from the back room smiling.

"I think you've picked a perfect cake." Mom turned to Miranda, "And you'll be happy to know it has pink roses on it too."

"Miranda invited me to a slumber party tomorrow, can I go?" I asked my mom in front of everyone because I knew she would be less likely to say no. She was still nervous about me hanging around with humdrums.

"A sleeping party? I suppose that would be fun. Will you wear hats?"

My face flushed red. "It's called a slumber party, Mom, and no one wears party hats."

"Of course. We'll pack up a box of cupcakes you can take over with you," Mom offered.

Miranda clapped her hands. I couldn't tell if she was excited that I got to come to her party or that I was bringing cupcakes.

Miranda pulled on my elbow and leaned into my ear to whisper while my mom and her cousin made arrangements about the cake. "I know you're friends with Katie, but I can't invite any more people over. I don't think you should tell her about the party."

My happy thoughts came to a sudden stop. I hadn't thought about Katie. I knew she didn't have any interest in being friends with Miranda. I agreed with her that Bethany and Paula weren't very nice, but I could tell Miranda wasn't like them. I didn't like the idea of keeping another secret from Katie, but it wasn't like she would want to go to the slumber party anyway. I chewed on the inside of my lip. It couldn't be that big of deal to keep a secret about something she wouldn't even be interested in if she knew.

"Okay. I won't tell her," I whispered back to Miranda.

Maybe it was all the frosting I had eaten earlier, or it might be the promise I had made Miranda, but my stomach felt turned upside-down.

seven

A dog:

   a. eats the same thing (kibble) for dinner every day

   b. doesn't wear any clothes

   c. can't open a door, make a sandwich, or fold a blanket by himself

   d. thinks fetch is the most interesting game ever

   e. *still* thinks he knows more than you

I had packed an overnight bag and was walking to Miranda's house with my pillow under my arm. I was trying to walk quickly so that Winston would get tired and go home, but he had the benefit of four legs so he could walk pretty fast.

"This is a bad idea," Winston puffed, his tongue hanging out.

"You already said that," I pointed out. "Like ten times."

"Why did you tell Katie you were spending the night at your grandma's?"

I hadn't meant to tell Katie anything. I figured I wouldn't have to lie to her about going to Miranda's if I just didn't tell her at all. Then Katie called and invited me over to her house to play Monopoly with her parents. I didn't know what to say. The lie about going to my grandma's came out of my mouth before I knew what happened.

It used to be that I didn't have any really good friends, and now I had too many. Being popular was really complicated. Katie was my best friend, but I still wanted to be friends with Miranda.

"I'm supposed to learn as much as I can about humdrums. Miranda is the most popular girl in my class. Going to her slumber party is almost like homework," I explained to Winston.

Winston raised one of his furry eyebrows. "Uh-huh."

"Katie would understand if she knew I was a fairy, but I can't tell her. There really wasn't anything else I could do."

"Everyone knows dogs are man's best friend, which makes me a friend expert. I can tell you this is most definitely NOT something someone does to a best friend."

"I'll tell Katie about it someday. Once Miranda and I are friends, I'll introduce the two of them and we can all hang out together." I stopped in front of Miranda's house. Suddenly I felt nervous. The only humdrum I'd ever hung out with was Katie.

"Why do you even want to be friends with Miranda?"

"I don't know, I just do," I said.

"'Never be distracted by a new squeaky is one of my mottos," Winston said. For a dog, he always was offering advice.

"What does that mean?"

"It means sometimes someone might offer you a shiny new squeaky toy, and it might *look* better than your old beat up fuzzy hot-dog toy, but that doesn't mean it is." Winston cocked his head to the side. "A few bites and the squeaker stops working."

"Are you comparing my friends to your disgusting chew toy?" My nose wrinkled up. I was always finding Winston's wet, ragged stuffed hot-dog toy in my bed.

"My stuffed hot dog is not disgusting." Winston was clearly offended. "All my wisdom is wasted. I thought finally when a person could understand me there would be progress. Now I find out you hear, but you don't listen."

"I listen, but I also have to do what I think is best." I glanced quickly at the house. I hoped that Miranda and her friends weren't looking out the window watching me talk to my dog. Most people only said sit or stay to their dog. Things were always more complicated with Winston. "I really have to go."

"Don't come crying to me when this goes badly." Winton turned and headed toward home.

I wasn't going to get mad. I shouldn't expect a dog to understand how complicated friendships could be. His closest friend was Louise, a cat, and when they fought, they chased each other around the yard until Louise whacked him on the nose with her paw.

Miranda's mom pointed me down the stairs to the family room. Miranda, Bethany, and Paula were sitting in a circle with a stack of magazines in the middle. When Miranda saw me she squealed and ran over to give me a hug. I unzipped my bag and pulled out the box of cupcakes my mom had promised.

"I was just telling everyone how you're a wedding

expert," Miranda said. "We're going to have the best time tonight!"

"Where's your sleeping bag?" Bethany asked.

I noticed the rest of them all had fancy sleeping bags. Miranda's was pink with peace signs all over it; Paula's was covered with rainbows; and Bethany's had a giant unicorn. Figures she would like unicorns. Unicorns looked pretty, but if you got on their wrong side they would chase you down and poke you with their horn. They tended to be more stuck-up than your average horse.

"I don't have a sleeping bag. I brought my pillow and a blanket," I said. It hadn't seemed like a big deal at home, but now I could tell it was a huge mistake.

Bethany rolled her eyes at Paula. "Whatever. I never met anyone who didn't have their own sleeping bag."

There was a moment of silence when no one knew what to say. The sleepover was not getting off to a good start.

"Now that everyone is here, I'll show you my dress," Miranda announced.

We squealed and followed her into her room. Her mom yelled that we had to wash our hands before we touched the dress. We sat lined up on Miranda's bed as she pulled it out of the closet.

After everything Miranda had said about the dress, I expected it to be fancier. It was pink satin, but the style was rather plain. It didn't have any lace or sparkles on it. There was a bow that tied in the back, but that was it. It seemed to me that the whole point of a wedding was to be as fancy as possible. She really needed to wear sparkly earrings.

"What do you think, Willow?" Miranda asked.

I stepped up as the official wedding expert and circled the dress. I pinched the fabric in my fingers. "The color is nice," I said. "Nice full skirt, the bow is a good size. This style is traditional." The beginning of an idea was starting in the back of my mind. I had an idea how I could make the wedding even better.

Bethany snorted. I could tell that she didn't think I was a wedding expert at all. I would show her.

eight

Fairy tales...

    a. are the only way that humdrums know about fairy godmothers anymore.

    b. should not be used to give you any ideas. Some of that stuff is just made up.

My first slumber party was not going very well. I could tell that Bethany and Paula didn't want me to be there. They made a big deal about how I don't like pepperoni on my pizza. I don't like to eat it even if the pepperoni is picked off—because everyone knows it leaks that pepperoni juice onto everything. They said everyone likes pepperoni, but you could tell what they meant is that everyone "normal" likes it. I felt a bit sick after dinner, but it wasn't the pizza. I wanted to go home, but it was only seven p.m. I still had the whole night and morning to get through. If I called my mom and asked her to pick me up, they would make fun of me after I left. They would say I was too much of a baby to handle a slumber party. It was bad being here, but it would be worse to go home.

After dinner we pulled on our pajamas and went downstairs. Everyone spread out their sleeping bags in a row, and I spent time arranging my blanket pile so that it looked as sleeping bag–like as possible. I was on the very end, as far away from Miranda as Bethany could stick me. If I wasn't careful I would roll into the fireplace. Miranda's living room clearly wasn't built for a four-person slumber party.

Miranda's parents were going to let us stay up as late as we wanted watching movies. Picking a movie was going to be hard because Miranda seemed to have every movie ever made. Even the old-fashioned, black-and-white kind. Bethany wanted to watch a romance. Paula liked scary movies. I excused myself while they were fighting about what to watch and snuck up to Miranda's room. The bridesmaid dress was hanging in a plastic bag on the back of the closet door. I slipped the plastic off and looked it over. Miranda would love this dress even more if it had more sparkle. This was my first chance to grant a wish. It was a wedding wish too, which made it a big deal. My parents would be superimpressed. My sister's first wish had been helping someone find a quarter for the parking meter. This was much cooler.

I quietly closed the bedroom door and took some deep breaths. I focused on the dress and did a magic spell.

Nothing happened.

I rolled up my pajama sleeves and tried again, this time squinting my eyes and *really* concentrating.

Nothing.

Magic was a lot harder than my parents made it look. Every fairy godmother had one magical skill that chose them, but everything else had to be learned. I bet my sister would know how to do this spell. She was always the top of her class. I pressed my mouth together and tried as hard as I could. I could tell my face was turning all red and sweat popped up on my forehead like I was running laps in gym. My body shook with the effort.

POP!

I fell back onto Miranda's bed panting. As soon as I got my breath back I jumped up so I could see how the dress turned out. My eyes swept up and down over the dress. It didn't look any different. That wasn't possible. Wait! There on the bottom of the skirt there was something. I picked it up and found one silver sequin on the very bottom of the hem of the skirt.

One sequin.

I sat back down on the bed. One sequin didn't make the dress sparkly. It looked like a mistake. At this rate it would take me all night, maybe a whole week, to make the dress over. I really wanted to grant Miranda's wish. I chewed on my lower lip and tried to think of a solution. If only all magic came as easy to me as talking to animals.

I snapped my fingers. That was it! I could be fairy godmother just like in the movie *Cinderella*. I dashed over to Miranda's window and opened it. I whistled to attract the attention of a robin that was sitting in the tree. I quickly explained the situation. I spoke to the robin in my head so that no one could overhear me. I preferred to talk out loud, but there are times you need to keep the conversation private. I needed the bird to get all his friends and maybe enlist the help of some mice to make over the dress. I stressed that they should keep the dress mostly the same, but that it needed some bling.

I left the window open and slipped out of the room. I had to fight the urge to dance down the stairs I was so excited. I was already imagining how excited Miranda would be when she saw the dress in the morning. I was starting to see how wish-granting could be really fun.

I hardly slept all night. Partly because I couldn't wait to see how the dress turned out, but also because Paula had picked a movie that was superscary. I was afraid that there might be zombies outside. The only good thing about zombies is that they didn't seem like they could run very fast. I was willing to bet that I could outrun them. I was 100 percent sure I could outrun Bethany. She always had a note from home on days we had to run laps in gym. She didn't like to get too sweaty. She would be a zombie snack for sure.

Miranda's mom called downstairs that it was time to get up. She was making pancakes for breakfast. I like pancakes—there's no pepperoni on them. Miranda got up first, and I held my breath when she went upstairs to her room. I wondered if she would cry with happiness when she saw it.

"AAAAHHH!!!" Miranda wailed.

The rest of us ran full speed to her room. I collided

with Bethany who had stopped right in the doorway. I turned to excuse myself, but when I saw the dress my mouth fell open. Holy moly.

The birds had made the dress something special all right. A garland of woven silver gum wrappers wound around the bottom of the dress. They had attached bottle caps along the neckline and there were Styrofoam noodles stuck everywhere. A few of the birds were standing on the windowsill chirping with pride.

"What do you think?" the robin asked. His chest feathers puffed out. "The bottle caps were my idea."

I swallowed hard. Either the fairy godmother in *Cinderella* had more fashionable birds help her or that part of the story was made up. The dress was ruined.

"Well. It *is* sparkly," I said to the birds. I didn't want to insult them. I could tell they'd done their best.

"No one will ever believe this was our first dress. I had no idea I had such a natural talent," the robin said.

"You always were a great nest maker," the other bird pointed out. "Remember the year you used floral twigs?"

"You certainly have a unique style," I managed to say.

"How did this happen?" Miranda moaned.

"Do you think it was zombies?" Paula asked, her voice shaking.

✯ 57 ✯

"I told you we shouldn't watch that movie," Bethany said. Miranda's mom pounded up the stairs to see what all the noise was about.

I thought Miranda's mom might scream when she saw the dress, but she just stood there with her mouth open. "H-h-how did this happen?" she stammered. "What did you girls do?"

"We didn't do it! It was like this when we got here," Miranda said. "The window was open. Someone must have broken in and done it."

Miranda's mom crossed her arms over her chest. "Do you expect me to believe that someone broke into this house and they didn't bother to steal anything? All they did was sneak in and mess with your dress. Look at it! It's ruined!"

"Well, that one has no sense of fashion," the robin huffed outside, clearly offended by the early reviews of the dress. The two birds flew off without another word.

Miranda's mom turned to face the rest of us. "I am shocked you girls would be a part of something like this. I think it would be best if you all called your parents and went home now." She stormed back downstairs, leaving us to look at one another.

It didn't sound to me like we were going to have any

pancakes. I felt terrible. All I'd wanted to do was make Miranda's dress special. Now I knew why my sister started with a simple parking meter wish.

Miranda was crying softly and Paula and Bethany were patting her on the back.

"It'll be okay," I said. I looked at the dress. The one good thing was the birds weren't the best seamstresses. Most things were just resting on top of the dress or tacked on with a single stitch. "I bet most of this stuff would come off pretty easy." I pulled a few bottle caps off the dress to show her. Paula leaped over and started helping me.

"What if my cousin decides that she doesn't want me in the wedding anymore?" Miranda wailed.

"She wouldn't take you out of the wedding because of the dress," Bethany said. "You can tell her it was some kind of accident."

"It's not just the dress," Miranda said. "Look at this." She opened her mouth and pointed to one of her front teeth. The three of us leaned in to look, but I couldn't tell what we were looking at. The tooth looked fine to me. Maybe her cousin didn't think she flossed often enough. "My tooth is loose!" Miranda said. "If I lose it before the wedding then I'll look goofy in all the photos."

"How come you're losing your tooth so late?" Bethany asked. "I lost mine ages ago." Paula and I both glared at her. It was obvious Miranda was upset enough without pointing out to her that everyone else had already lost all their front teeth.

"Would your cousin really kick you out of the wedding?" Paula whispered.

"My mom keeps talking about how pictures last a lifetime and how I'm too young to be a bridesmaid anyway. No one wants a toothless junior bridesmaid."

"You should stay away from apples," Paula offered.

"And gum too," Bethany suggested. "Nothing too chewy and always eat on the other side of your mouth. Maybe if you don't use the tooth at all between now and the wedding it will stay in place."

"Girls! It's time for you to head home," Miranda's mom yelled up the stairs.

"Thanks for inviting me," I said to Miranda.

"We never had these kinds of problems at our parties until we invited you," Bethany said, as she stomped past me.

I would have gotten mad, except Bethany was right. What happened was my fault. I hadn't meant for the dress to be ruined. I went downstairs and called my mom to let her know I would be walking home early. I folded up my blanket and left. Miranda didn't come out of her room.

Winston was waiting for me on the sidewalk outside. He must have overheard my conversation with my mom.

"Don't say anything," I said, as I turned to walk home.

"Not even an I-told-you-so?" Winston fell into step with me. "What happened anyway?"

"It was a wish-granting complication."

"A complication?" Winston raised his furry eyebrows.

"It was a bit more than a complication. It'll be okay. I figured out how I can make it right."

Winston chewed on the hem of my jeans to make me stop. "Wait a minute. I'm not sure this is a good idea. Maybe you should leave the wish-granting to grown-ups."

"How am I ever going to learn how to grant wishes if I can't make a simple wedding wish work out well? The wish wasn't even for the bride! Besides, I know what to do now." I walked quickly. I was going to need to talk to my grandmother. Even though I knew what I needed to do, I wasn't exactly sure how to do it. I might have screwed up the dress wish, but I was going to find a way to tackle Miranda's tooth problem. "Don't worry. For this wish I'm going to get help."

"Who?" Winston asked.

I stopped. "I'm going straight to the top. The Tooth Fairy."

nine

The Tooth Fairy . . .

    a. contrary to popular belief, wears a business suit.

    b. is a whiz at math and economics.

    c. isn't known for her sense of humor.

    d. is all business.

My grandma's house is awesome. It's a stone cottage right on the river and surrounded by trees. Her garden in the back is wild with flowers and bushes. The inside of the house is stuffed with things she had brought back from her travels around the world. She especially liked to collect magical items. On a table there might be a carved marble cat from Egypt next to a pile of casting stones from Scotland. You had to be careful about what you touched. Once Lucinda was playing with one of grandma's porcelain swans from China and it came to life. It got feathers everywhere until my grandma turned it back.

"All right then, who would like a snack?" Grandma pushed the swinging door from her kitchen open with her hip. She was carrying a giant tray with cups and cookies and a giant bone. A pot of hot chocolate floated behind her, trailing steam like a streamer. Winston's tail picked up speed, thumping on the carpet.

"Do you think the bone is for me?" Winston asked.

"Well, I'm sure it's not for me," I told him. Grandma placed the bone on a silver serving tray on the floor. She tucked a plaid napkin into Winston's collar and then sat across from me.

"Are you a bit chilly?" She snapped her fingers and a fire roared to life in the fireplace. She passed me the cookies while the pot of hot chocolate poured itself into our cups. "I like fall. It gives a person an excuse to get cozy. Now, tell me what brings you by for a visit."

I took a sip of the hot chocolate and tucked my feet underneath me in the chair. I told her all about what happened with the bridesmaid dress. Her lips twitched like she might laugh, but she didn't. This is why you can tell your grandma anything.

"Birds are very unreliable," I said, to prove I had learned my lesson.

"At least in the fashion department," Grandma agreed. "Did you want me to make sure Miranda's dress is okay?"

"That would be great." I fidgeted in my seat. I was glad Grandma could fix the dress, but I still wanted to help with the wedding.

"Go on, tell her your big plan to negotiate with the Tooth Mafia," Winston said.

Grandma couldn't tell what he said since she didn't speak dog, but she knew his woof meant something. "Sounds like there might be more to the story. Is there something else you wanted to ask me?"

I glared at Winston. If he thought I was going to play fetch with him later, he was wrong. For a small dog, he had a big mouth.

"Miranda is afraid she might lose her tooth before the wedding. It's a big deal. I wanted to grant her wish to keep it, at least a little while longer. After what happened with the dress I thought I better get some help." Who knew what might happen if I tried to fix the tooth on my own. All of Miranda's teeth might fall out, or the loose tooth could grow twenty times its size until she looked like a walrus.

"I'm afraid there isn't anything we can do. Fairy godmothers can't do everything. Teeth are outside our control. I can promise you that Miranda will be in the wedding. Her cousin won't change her mind." Grandma winked at me.

"I was thinking I could talk to the Tooth Fairy," I said.

Grandma's cup rattled against her saucer. She put her cup down on the table. "The Tooth Fairy? Are you sure that's something you want to do?"

Tooth fairies were a different division of fairy world. According to our fairy history books, centuries ago a fairy godfather, Colin McNary, was put in charge of tooth wishes. He handpicked his team. He only wanted fairies with top-of-the-line math skills so they could figure out what they were supposed to leave for each tooth. He was so picky about who could be on the tooth team that eventually you had to be born into a family that descended from his original team. Each tooth fairy was assigned a location they were responsible for maintaining. You could always tell who was a tooth fairy because they dressed like lawyers on top with suit blazers and briefcases and then flouncy tulle ballerina skirts on bottom. They always went places in a rush, and they liked to sort out exactly how much to leave for each tooth by pulling out their calculators. I didn't know for sure, but it was rumored they could do long division in their head—and not easy problems either. They had the strongest magical abilities of any fairy. I still wouldn't want to be one because they had to touch people's old teeth, and I thought that sounded kinda yucky.

"Why do tooth fairies have such strong magic?" I asked.

Grandma leaned back into her armchair. "A long, long, time ago fairy godmothers and tooth fairies had the same level of magic. As to why their magic has stayed so strong, while ours has gotten weaker, no one knows for sure."

"Maybe it's something with the teeth," I suggested.

"I don't think it's the teeth. I think it's because so many people believe in the Tooth Fairy, it keeps their magic strong. Most humdrums believe in the tooth fairies for years longer than they believe in us."

"So believing is what keeps the magic going?" I asked.

"Maybe." Grandma poured more hot chocolate for both of us. "Now what are you hoping to do by talking to the Tooth Fairy? They take their schedules very seriously, you know. When it's time for a tooth to go, it goes. They have everyone's teeth on a spreadsheet."

"I was hoping that I could explain to the Tooth Fairy how important it is that Miranda hang on to that particular tooth for just a bit longer. It could fall out right after the wedding."

"I'm not sure she'll be open to changing her schedule to grant a wish," Grandma said.

"Maybe I could make a deal with her. I could polish her tooth collection or organize all of her paperwork." Fairies had to file form 15.4.2: Permission to Enter a Humdrum Home and Remove Belongings. This meant every time they collected a tooth, they had to file a form. It was a long form too, and you had to make three copies. That's a lot of filing. I was hoping the tooth fairy assigned to Miranda would be the kind to be behind with her paperwork.

"No one will ever say that you wish small," Grandma said with a laugh. "You know even most Fairy Godmother Level 3s don't try and mess with tooth fairies."

I sighed. I knew what I wanted to do was almost impossible. "I know, but the worst that will happen is that she'll say no. And if she says yes, then I'm able

"Sorry to break up this very touching moment. Can someone please do something about the way I look? I am not a bell- or glitter-coated type of dog. I am a very serious dog, who would appreciate looking like one."

POP!

The bells and glitter were gone. Winston was wearing a tiny black pinstriped suit with a hole for his tail and a fedora.

"Is this supposed to be funny?" Winston asked.

Grandma and I looked at each other and burst out laughing.

ten

True or False:

George Washington had a fairy godfather.

Answer:

Duh. True. How else do you think he got across the Delaware River?

History was not my best subject at Riverside Elementary. My problem was that at the Fairy Academy we learned the same history, but we focused on how fairy godmothers and fairy godfathers were involved. For example, Thomas Jefferson had a really hard time writing the Declaration of Independence. This is understandable because it's a pretty important document. It's not like writing a grocery list where if you forget to put down a reminder to get cheese it will be a pain, but not a real problem. (Unless you were planning to have grilled cheese for dinner.) If you are writing a document that will make a whole nation free, you don't want to leave any of the important bits out.

Thomas Jefferson's fairy godfather was named Seamus Winkles. He had a very funny last name, but he did a great job on the Declaration. The part about all men being created equal? That was all Seamus's doing. He also added the line about pursuing happiness being a right. Seamus was a very good writer.

Then there was Lucille King, Fairy Godmother Level 3, who helped the Apollo 11 mission land on the moon. Talk about complicated. We had whole chapters in our history books devoted to how this was the first time wishes had been granted in zero gravity.

It's hard to pass a history class when you can't remember the humdrum name involved and there wouldn't be any extra credit points for knowing the fairy godmother. We were learning all about the Revolutionary War in class. Ms. Caul broke the class up into groups to work on a project.

Our group was going to make a map of how the United States looked back at the time of the war. We picked Katie to draw the outline of the map because she was the best artist in our class. Katie started by look-ing at the map in our textbook and then measuring the blank paper. She made small marks in pencil with her ruler.

"What's taking so long? The rest of us have stuff to do too, you know," Bethany complained.

"I have to make sure where everything goes before I start or else Maine will be huge, and there won't be any room for New Hampshire." Katie explained.

"Well, we better have time for me to do my part." Bethany had volunteered to draw horses on our map. She said it was because George Washington liked horses, but we all knew it was because she was horse crazy. She had horses and unicorns on everything. I don't want to be mean or anything, but even though Bethany thought she was great at drawing horses, she really wasn't. Her horses all looked like cows. Cows with knobby knees.

"You can help me draw some horses if you want," Bethany told Nathan.

"Nah. I'd rather draw the buildings."

Bethany glared at me. It wasn't my fault that Nathan wanted to draw buildings with me instead of her stupid cow horses.

"Nobody will get to draw anything if I don't get this map right." Katie started to outline the map. She stopped every few moments to check the pencil marks on the page and to consult our textbook.

"Everybody give her some space," I waved my arms to clear some room around the table for Katie to work.

"It's a shame Katie wasn't at the slumber party this weekend with the rest of us. She could have helped draw people's wedding dresses." Bethany slapped her hand over her mouth as if the words had fallen out by accident. "Whoops. I forgot I wasn't supposed to mention you were at the party."

Katie turned to me. "What does she mean? I thought you were at your grandma's on Saturday."

"Um. I was going to go, but I ended up going there on Sunday instead." I crossed my fingers hoping that Katie would let things drop there.

"So on Saturday night you were at Miranda's slumber party?" Katie dropped her marker making a big black dot on our map paper.

"Sort of. I was going to tell you." Everyone in our work group was silent watching Katie and me. Bethany was smiling.

"When?" Katie demanded.

"I didn't say anything because I knew you weren't interested in all the wedding stuff anyway. I went because Miranda wanted to show me her dress."

Katie's mouth was a straight line. I could tell she was really mad. "I can't believe you lied to me."

"If we don't finish this map soon we're not going to get our project done," Nathan said. He was the only one who didn't seem interested in all the drama.

Katie grabbed the pen and rushed through the rest of the map. It didn't look very much like the United States. It looked more like an oozing outline of a fried egg.

"There's your map." Katie nearly threw the pen down onto the table. She sat down in her seat and crossed her arms over her chest.

"I'll start on my horses now," Bethany said. "Nathan, you can draw some buildings near them because they'll need a stable."

Nathan sighed and I thought I heard him mumble "girls" to Ryan, who was the only other guy working in our group.

"Are you mad?" I whispered to Katie.

She didn't look over. She stared straight ahead.

"I was going to tell you. I really was." She still

wouldn't look at me. "I didn't even have that good of a time," I said quietly so only she could hear me. "You'll never guess what kind of sleeping bag Bethany has." When she didn't answer I kept talking. "It has unicorns all over it." I snorted to show what I thought of a unicorn-covered sleeping bag.

"You shouldn't talk about your best friends like that," Katie said still looking straight ahead.

"Bethany isn't my best friend. You are."

Katie turned to look at me. "Really? I never would have guessed."

eleven

Reasons to not invite a humdrum over to my house:

    a. A framed picture of my mom and dad on their honeymoon riding the Loch Ness Monster hangs in the dining room.

    b. The magic mirror in the bathroom is always giving advice on what to wear. (Warning: The mirror isn't crazy about bright colors or plaids.)

    c. They could catch my dog, Winston, playing chess with Louise the cat while the school hamster, Lester, acts as referee.

    d. My sister could fly by, which means explaining that both a) she can shrink down to Tinkerbell size, and b) she can fly.

    e. About fifty zillion reasons that I don't have time to list.

★ ★ ★

Katie was really mad. She didn't talk to me the rest of the day. When history was over I slid a piece of gum onto her desk, cinnamon flavored, her favorite. She picked it up between two fingers like it was a squished worm and offered it to Ryan. When the final bell rang Katie pulled on her giant yellow rubber boots and left without waiting for me.

It was raining. Katie was stomping home through the puddles. I hadn't remembered to wear my rain boots that morning. I said a quick spell to keep my socks dry and then ran after her down the sidewalk

"Katie! Wait!" I yelled. When she didn't stop I caught up to her and grabbed her jacket. "I want to talk to you."

Katie yanked her arm back. "I have to get home. I have to feed Crackers."

"I could help," I offered even though her bird sometimes bit.

"I'm not sure my mom will let me have anyone over." Katie didn't meet my eyes. We both knew that her mom never seemed to mind me coming over before. "Maybe you should go over to Miranda's house instead."

"Don't be mad," I said. "I don't want to go to Miranda's.

I just wanted to go to her slumber party to see what it would be like. Don't you ever want to see what it would be like to be popular?"

"No." Katie pulled on the hood of her jacket to keep the rain off her face. "I should go." She started walking down the street again.

I chased after her. "How can I make it up to you? Do you want to borrow my pink sweater?" Katie didn't even turn around. "Or you could *have* my pink sweater. I know it's your favorite." I hated the idea of giving up my pink sweater. It was fuzzy and not even remotely itchy. However, Katie was my best friend.

"I don't want your sweater," Katie said walking straight through a deep puddle.

"What if I let you borrow Winston? We could take him for a walk in the park and if anyone asks you can say he's your dog." I hoped Winston would agree to go along with that plan. "Or if you want, I could bring you some cookies from my mom's bakery. I can bring the toffee kind with chocolate chips." Katie still didn't say anything. The toffee cookies were the best too. "I could bring the cookies while they're still warm," I said.

Katie stopped. "I don't want your things or to borrow your dog or even cookies!"

I took a step back. I could tell I was going to start crying. I had blown my first humdrum friendship. "You don't want to be my best friend anymore, do you?"

"That's not fair," Katie said. "You say you want to be my best friend, but you keep secrets from me all the time."

"No, I don't," I protested.

"You didn't tell me about the slumber party. You didn't tell me about Nathan liking you. There are all kinds of things you don't tell me. And how come I've never been to your house?" Katie crossed her arms over her chest.

"It's not that you can't come over, it's just that I think hanging at your place is more fun," I said.

"What if *I* think hanging at *your* place would be more fun?" Katie fired back.

I pressed my lips together. I couldn't come up with a good reason why Katie couldn't come over. There was no way to tell her the truth that my family was just too weird.

Katie noticed that I wasn't saying anything. "See? You don't want me to come over." She started walking away again.

I grabbed her arm before she could go too far. "I'll

talk to my mom and see if you can come over later this week." There was no way I could invite her to come right now. There was some major preparation work I was going to have to do before she could even come past the front door.

"Really? You're inviting me over?" Katie asked.

I swallowed the lump in my throat and nodded. "Yep."

Katie touched my shoulder. "You know you don't have to worry about your house. It doesn't need to be fancy or anything."

I tried to smile. "I know. It's more my family. They're . . ." I wasn't sure how to even begin to explain them. "My family is sort of quirky."

"I'll like them because I like you," Katie said.

"I'll talk to my mom tonight," I promised.

Katie smiled, then looked down. "That's weird. Look at your legs."

I glanced down. My pants were wet where the rain had soaked in, but a few inches below my knees all the way to my shoes was bone dry. Uh-oh. I hadn't thought about how the dry sock spell would look. "Well, I should let you go so you can feed Crackers. She must be getting hungry." I backed away.

"How are you staying dry?"

"Oh, special socks. My mom orders them from place that specializes in socks for swimming." As soon as the story was out of my mouth, I knew it didn't make any sense.

"Socks for swimming? I never heard of anything like that." Katie's face was scrunched up with disbelief.

"You wouldn't want Crackers to get too hungry. She's already a pretty thin bird." I took a few more steps toward my house.

"Wait, can I see your socks up close?" Katie called.

"Gotta go! I'll see you tomorrow!" I yelled over my shoulder before running home. Hopefully she wouldn't notice that my legs stayed dry as I splashed through the puddles.

twelve

True or False:

Ten years old is old enough to have your own phone in your room.

Answer:

True. Unless you have my parents, in which case the answer is false.

I was the only one in our house that ever answered the humdrum phone. Any fairies calling our house used the holo-phone that created a holographic image of the fairy calling you. It's nice because you can see the person calling you, but this is a downside if you are still in your jammies when they call. The only people who call our humdrum phone are people trying to sell us carpet cleaning and Katie. I tried to convince my parents that I should be allowed to have the humdrum phone in my room, but so far they weren't convinced. They didn't think anyone who was ten needed their own phone. Which goes to show you they don't really remember being ten at all.

I ran downstairs when I heard the humdrum phone ring. "Hello, Doyle residence."

"Hi, Willow," Grandma said.

"Why did you call this phone?" I asked in surprise. Grandma always used the holo-phone before. Maybe she was in her jammies and didn't want us to see her. I don't know why she'd think that, though. She had a great bathrobe made from a Japanese kimono. If I had pajamas like that I would wear them everywhere. Mine were flannel with purple sheep.

"I called this phone because I wanted to talk to you without your parents knowing."

I looked over my shoulder to make sure no one was listening to our conversation. My sister was in the living room doing her homework, but I could count on her to ignore me. "What's up? Were you able to get in touch with," I looked over my shoulder again, "you know, the TF?"

"I did. After a bit of checking around I found out

the fairy in charge of Miranda's neighborhood is Phyllis McMillan," Grandma said. "I should warn you, she's pretty serious, even for a tooth fairy. She wears three watches so she's never late for an appointment."

"What did she say about the tooth?" Maybe I would get lucky and she would tell us that Miranda's tooth wasn't due to fall out for weeks.

"It's scheduled to fall out the night before the wedding."

This was a disaster. "What are we going to do?" I whispered in the phone. "We have to do something."

"I set up a meeting for you to talk to her," Grandma said.

"Me?" My voice came out high and squeaky. "Why would she listen to me? I'm only a sprite. I'm not even the top of my sprite class. Isn't she more likely to help you?"

"I don't think Ms. McMillan is the type of tooth fairy who's very impressed by rank. She's worked with plenty of Fairy Godmothers Level 3. I think what might make a difference is if you explain why it's important. This is one of your first wish-grants. For you this is personal. That might impress her."

I didn't say anything. I knew grandma thought I was

pretty special, but I wasn't sure that this tooth fairy was going to agree. My grandma was always saying things like how she liked my hair, even when my mom cut it and it was sort of uneven and my bangs were too short. Grandmas always think your art is the best even when they can't tell what it's supposed to be. Grandmas are like that.

"Do you want to meet with her? She's agreed to come to my house and talk with you on Friday night."

"I don't know," I said. Talking to the tooth fairy had seemed like a good idea, but now that it was really going to happen, it was scary.

"It's up to you, Willow. If you don't want to, you don't have to."

I sighed. Now the success of the wedding was completely up to me. Being in charge of a Happily Ever After (or at least a no-toothless-smile-photo problem) seemed like a lot for me to handle. "Okay, I'll try."

I could hear Grandma clap her hands. "Perfect! I'll make some tea and scones for your meeting. Not to worry. There will be chocolate milk, too."

I was going to be too nervous to eat. I could tell already. Now, in addition to sorting out what do about Katie, I had to get ready to negotiate with a tooth fairy.

For someone in the fourth grade I had a lot to handle. No wonder I'd started chewing on my fingernails again. All this worry couldn't be good for me. It might stunt my growth. I was going to end up short with icky nails. If I had to go it alone with the Tooth Fairy, maybe Grandma could help me with my other problem.

"Can I ask you something? Katie wants to come over to my house." I said. "Do you think I should invite her over?" I realized I was chewing on my thumbnail, so I pulled it out of my mouth.

"Hmm. This doesn't seem too tricky. Do you want her to come visit?" Grandma asked.

"I *want* her to come, but I don't know if she *should* come over. What if she notices our house is so different than everybody else's?" I looked around the room. My sister had her spell textbook floating in front of her face so she could easily read it while she mixed a potion. The glass beaker belched out a plume of pink smoke that sparkled before it disappeared.

"Katie is friends with you. She doesn't want to go to another girl's house," Grandma said.

"But what if she figures out we're fairy?" I asked, as my dad walked past me on his way into the kitchen carrying a speckled dragon's egg under his arm.

"Pfft, a whole lot of worry about what would happen if humdrums knew without even knowing if it would be a big deal," Grandma said, blowing off my concerns.

"But it's against the rules to tell a humdrum! I could get in huge trouble if I told her."

"Of course you shouldn't *tell* her, but I also wouldn't run your life worrying about how she might find out. If you want her to come over, then you should invite her. She's not just a humdrum—she's your best friend. I know Katie from school, and she's pretty special. Almost as special as you."

I rolled my eyes. "You're my grandma, you have to think I'm special."

"But I'm also right. I'll see you on Friday."

I hung up the phone. Now all I had to do was convince my parents this was a good idea.

thirteen

An after-school snack could be:
   a. apple slices
   b. cookies
   c. ice cream
   d. cheese and crackers
   e. brownies; a red velvet three-layer cake with cream cheese icing; a dozen chocolate chip cookies; a dozen oatmeal cookies (six with raisins, six without); a fruit bowl complete with strawberries, pineapple, cherries and pieces of melon; a full veggie tray complete with ranch dip; small mini pizzas made with English muffins; and a pot of hot chocolate with marshmallows

Yep. My mom has gone overboard.

★ ★ ★

We had a big family meeting last night about Katie being allowed to come over to our house. My sister, Lucinda, was dead set against the plan, but I couldn't tell if it was because she didn't like me to get anything I wanted or if it was because she was scared of humdrums. It's like spiders. My sister says she isn't scared, but if she comes across one she gets all wiggy. I don't mind spiders. It's not their fault they're kind of creepy looking. People don't mind ladybugs. It seems unfair to not like another bug just because it's unlucky enough to be unattractive. I think people would like spiders much better if we were allowed to dress them up. Would you want to squish something that was wearing a bright blue polka-dotted bow with small black patent leather shoes? Me neither. Once I reach Sprite Level 3 and was allowed to do more animal magic, I fully planned to try out my spider dress-up plan.

I convinced my parents to let Katie come over by pointing out that not having her over was a bigger risk. Humdrums always invited their friends over. If I didn't invite Katie then she was more likely to figure out that

EILEEN COOK

something about me was strange. I could tell my mom was nervous, but my dad sort of liked the idea. He kept talking about how he hadn't spent any real face-to-face time with humdrums in a long time. I made him promise not to tell any jokes. Sometimes my dad thinks he's being funny, but it's just embarrassing. Last year at the Fairy Academy Parent Night he kept telling the same knock-knock joke.

> Knock knock
>
> Who's there?
>
> Fairy
>
> Fairy who?
>
> I am fairy good with magic—how about you?

Then if the person didn't laugh he would try and explain the joke, how "fairy" and "very" rhymed and he's very good with magic. It was awful. If you ever

have to explain a joke in order for people to understand why it might be funny, then it isn't really funny.
That should be a rule.

My parents and I spent hours the night before,
going through the house either putting things away
or enchanting them so Katie wouldn't see them at all.
Lucinda got really angry because we hid her project
for school that had an orange that turned into a small
coach. She'd made a whole diorama with buildings
made out of sugar cubes. She was really proud of it,
but it took up almost the whole dining room table. We
could have left it out, but she hadn't gotten the magic
with the orange quite right so it tended to pop between
being a fruit and a coach sort of willy-nilly. My mom
came up with the idea putting the diorama in the spare
bedroom. Lucinda stomped up to her room because
she didn't think she should have to move something
just because my friend was coming over. Older sisters
think everything should go their way all the time.

All day at school I kept thinking about Katie coming
over. I was excited to show her my room, but I was also
really nervous because I wanted things to go well. Katie
walked home with me after school.

"I'm looking forward to meeting your sister," Katie said.

"She's not very exciting." I wasn't actually sure if Lucinda would come out of her room. She tended to sulk when things didn't go her way. I think she thought that not having her around was a punishment. As far as I was concerned, she could stay in her room forever. I liked it.

"I always wished I had a sister. I'd even settle for having a brother," Katie said swinging her school bag as she walked.

"Are you kidding? You're so lucky to be an only child. Sisters are a pain," I told her.

"But there would always be someone around to hang out with."

I looked at Katie. For someone so smart she had some big gaps in her knowledge. "Older sisters never want to hang out. Mostly they yell at you for touching their stuff and then they slam the door in your face." I stopped in front of my house.

"Wow. I didn't know your dad had redone the yard again. I guess I haven't walked by in a while," Katie said. My dad loved the yard. He was always making our bushes into something different. For a long time we had a giant evergreen dragon with a spray of bright red geraniums shooting out of its mouth like fire. Right now he had shaped the bushes to look like a pack of dogs running across the yard with a bunch of white flowers in the shape of a giant bone down by the sidewalk. Sometimes humdrums in our neighborhood came by to take pictures. I tried to tell my dad that our yard didn't help us fit in with the regular humdrum world at all, but there was no convincing him.

"My dad likes gardening, he's always doing something," I explained. I opened the front door and jumped. My mom and dad were standing in the foyer waiting for us. Dad was wearing a suit and Mom had on her fancy poodle skirt that flared out from the waist. So much for them acting casual.

"Welcome to our home," Mom said.

Katie looked a bit surprised to see them standing there. Then my dad stepped forward and saluted Katie. He *saluted* her. I wanted to bury my face in my hands. This is why I never had people over.

"She isn't a general, Dad," I said.

Dad gave a hearty laugh like he had been joking, but I could tell the laugh was fake. "Well, of course not. She's not old enough to be a general."

"Would you girls like an after-school snack?" Mom offered, changing the subject before my dad decided that Katie was only old enough to be a private or maybe a sergeant.

"Thank you, Mrs. Doyle," Katie said. "That would be very nice." She was very polite when grown-ups were around. I could tell my mom liked her manners.

We filed into the dining room and I dropped my school bag when I saw the table. My mom had gone waaaaaaaaaaaaaay overboard. The table was covered, every inch, with snacks. There were cupcakes and a three layer cake. She had a watermelon carved to look like a swan that was full of slices and cubes of other fruit. There were cookies, brownies, bowls of M&M's separated by color, cheese, crackers, veggies cut up and a crystal bowl with ranch dip. In the center of the table she had a chocolate fountain with marshmallows, bananas, and strawberries on sticks so that you could stick them into the fountain and coat them with the chocolate.

"Wow," Katie said, her eyes as big as dinner plates.

My mom held out a banana on a stick. "Do you like chocolate?"

"Um, sure." Katie took the banana and stuck it into the fountain. "I never knew anyone who had a chocolate fountain in their house before." She looked around the room.

I glared at my mom, hoping she could tell that I thought she had gone too far. "My mom helps organize weddings, so this stuff is just a bunch of leftovers," I said trying to explain. "We don't usually have this much food around."

"Right. Of course not. These are leftovers," my mom repeated, wringing her hands.

"Why don't we make up a plate of stuff and go to my room," I suggested. I grabbed a cupcake and a bunch of grapes. Katie picked up a plate and looked around the table, trying to decide.

Dad whipped out his notebook and began to scribble in it. "Interesting," he said when she selected a piece of red velvet cake. His eyebrows shot up when she took some strawberries. "Did you notice that the first two things you picked were red foods? Is red your favorite color?"

Katie looked down in surprise at her plate. "I didn't notice they were both red. Purple is my favorite color."

"Interesting." Dad scribbled more in his notebook. "I know there aren't any purple foods, but if there were, would you be more likely to pick them?"

"Actually, eggplant is purple," Katie pointed out.

Dad snapped his fingers making both Katie and me jump. "Excellent point! Do you like eggplant?"

"No. I'll eat it if my mom puts enough cheese on it, but I don't like it." Katie paused to think. "The color doesn't really make a difference. I don't like it because it sort of tastes like a funny mushy potato."

"Let's go to my room," I grabbed Katie by the elbow before my dad could ask any more goofy questions. We climbed to the top of the stairs and bumped into Lucinda, who was headed into her room.

"You must be Willow's sister!" Katie said.

Lucinda backed up quickly until she hit the wall. She slid along the hallway keeping the maximum distance between Katie and herself. She was totally freaked out to be that close to a humdrum, I could see it in her eyes. As far as she was concerned, Katie was as scary as a big hairy spider in the bathtub.

"I'm her best friend from school, Katie." She held out her hand to shake Lucinda's.

"AAAAAH! Don't touch me!" Lucinda ran the rest of the way down the hall, stopping in her bedroom doorway to look back at us. Then she slammed the door.

"Well, that's my sister," I said, shrugging. Katie looked at me. "I warned you older sisters are weird."

I walked the rest of the way down the hall to my room. Winston was sitting on the bed. He had seen everything that had happened in the hall.

"Well, it looks like this visit is going well so far," Winston said. "It's a wonder you haven't had her visit before now."

fourteen

True or False:

If someone sees you talking to the dog, they won't think it's weird.

Answer:

Generally true, unless they catch you having a full discussion with the dog where they can hear only one side, in which case they will decide you are the strangest person they've ever met.

Katie and I were doing a craft project in my room. Her mom had gotten her a book that showed how to make animals with small cotton pom-poms and pipe cleaners. So far we'd made a lion and giraffe. The lion looked pretty good, but the giraffe's neck kept drooping. Katie had gotten bored of following the directions and was now making up her own animals. She glued three pom-poms onto the neck of one creature.

"This is going to be a three-headed dog," she said. "It's like the one in *Harry Potter*, only instead of being scary, it's a friendly dog."

Winston snorted from the bed where he was watching everything. "Someone should tell her the dog in *Harry Potter* is totally made up. Three-headed dogs." He snorted again. "Absurd. Why mess with a perfect creature like a dog? We're naturally handsome. Of course some of us are more handsome than others."

I ignored Winston. "Look, I made a snake." I held up a pipe cleaner I had bent into an *S* shape. Katie and I laughed. I felt the tight band of tension that had been around my chest since we got to the house start to loosen up. Things were going to be okay.

That's when I saw my dad. I dropped my pipe cleaner snake.

My dad was floating right outside my window peeking in. He still had this notebook with him, and he was taking notes on how Katie played. His glasses had slid down to the end of his nose. What was he thinking? How was he going to explain being outside the second-floor window if Katie saw him? I flicked my hand at him, trying to let him know he needed to go away. Dad waved back.

Katie started to turn to see what I was looking at. I leaped up, nearly tripping over our school bags and lunged to the window, yanking the curtains closed with a quick swipe.

"Is it too bright in here? I think there might be too much sun," I leaned against the wall trying to look normal. I was breathing hard. "Wouldn't want to get a sunburn while sitting inside."

Katie stood. "It's not too bright. We need the light if we're going to see." She reached over to open the curtains.

"NO!" I screamed.

The curtains opened, but there was nothing there. My dad was down in the yard holding his hedge trimmers. He must have floated down right after I saw him.

Katie gave me a puzzled glance, but then she caught sight of a glass box of rainbow-colored pixie dust on my desk.

"Hey! You have a bunch of glitter." Katie picked up the pixie dust. "We can use this on our animals."

My heart froze. There was no telling what could happen if Katie spread that dust around. Winston could turn into an elephant; lime green snow could fall from the ceiling; or a thunderstorm could break out in the closet. The bed could float, the carpet could turn to water, or she could disappear. Careless use of pixie dust can cause all sorts of problems.

"I need that, um, glitter for a project," I said, my mouth completely dry. I held my hand out to take the glass box from her. I hoped she wouldn't notice how my hand was shaking.

"I'll just use a bit to stick on the noses of my three-headed dog." Katie started to twist off the top of the box.

I dove across the room, snatching the box out of Katie's hand. I hit the floor hard and rolled to a stop. I slowly opened my hand. The lid was still on the box. I took a deep breath. I felt a wave of relief until I looked up and saw the way Katie was looking at me.

"You must really need to use that glitter for something else," Katie said.

"Sorry. It's just that I promised my mom I would use it for a project I'm doing with her. She's sort of funny about her glitter," I said. I hoped Katie wouldn't say that since I'd basically just tackled her to get the box back, maybe *I* was the one who was weird about my craft supplies.

"I'm going to the bathroom," Katie said.

I started to follow her down the hall. I wanted to make sure the mirror kept its mouth shut. Katie stopped part way down the hall. I realized she probably thought it was strange I was going with her.

"I'm just making sure you know where the bathroom is," I said. I pointed to the bathroom, which was sort of dumb. It wasn't like our upstairs is that big.

Lucinda opened her bedroom door when she heard us in the hallway and peeked out. When she saw Katie, she dashed across the hall and threw herself in front of the closed spare room door as if Katie was trying to attack it with an axe.

"You can't go in here!" Lucinda said. "This room is off limits. No hum—er, no guests allowed."

"Okay. I was just going to the bathroom," Katie explained. She backed away from my sister.

"The guest room is a bit messy, so we don't let guests see it," I said. "It's sort of a non-guest, guest room."

Katie slipped into the bathroom and shut the door behind her.

"Stop acting like such a spaz," I hissed to Lucinda.

"What if she had seen the room? How were you planning to explain my orange carriage to her?" Lucinda whispered back. "Having a humdrum in this house is a big mistake. There's too many ways she can figure out we're fairies."

"She's not going to figure it out." I flounced back to my room.

Winston was surprised to see me back so quickly. He had a pipe cleaner in his mouth.

"Winston!" I yelled. I yanked the cleaner out of his mouth. All that was left was the wire center. The soft fluffy bit had been chewed off. I held the wet, bent wire in front of his face.

"It was on the floor," Winston pointed out. "You know how I find things on the floor irresistible." His tail drooped. I hardly ever yelled at him.

I sat on the floor next to Winston and picked through our craft stuff, putting things away. I had the sense Katie was going to want to go home soon. "At least you didn't eat Katie's three-headed dog. That's about the only thing that hasn't gone wrong."

"It will be okay. Real friends don't expect things to be perfect," Winston said, resting his muzzle on my knee. "Friends like you just the way you are. Even if you do, for example, sometimes chew on things you shouldn't."

"I'm not really mad at you for chewing on the pipe

cleaners. I just wanted Katie's visit to go well. How are we ever going to be best friends if I can never have her over here?"

"Maybe having people over takes practice. The first time you do anything it's always harder," Winston said. "Next time she comes over, your mom will know not to make quite so many snacks. Lucinda could maybe spend the afternoon with your grandmother."

I picked at the carpet. "I don't think Katie's ever going to want to come over again. Even if she did, I'm not sure if Mom and Dad will let her. We can't take the risk that she'll find out who we really are."

"What do you mean, who you really are?"

I spun around. Katie was standing in the doorway looking at me. Uh-oh. This was going to be harder to explain than the chocolate fountain.

fifteen

Positive of having a best friend with a great imagination:
She can always think of something fun to do.

Negative of having a best friend with a great imagination:
She can always think of something to explain what has happened, and her ideas are wild enough that it is just a matter of time before she figures out you're a fairy.

I stared at Katie, not sure what to say.

"Who are you talking to?" Katie asked.

"Um. Winston," I said fidgeting on the floor.

Winston's tail wagged lightly. I could have kicked myself. I could talk to Winston inside my head, but sometimes I talked to him out loud without thinking about it. It never occurred to me that Katie would be back so quickly from the bathroom. "I talk to him all the time. Just like you talk to Crackers."

"I don't pause after I speak to let her answer me," Katie pointed out. "We don't have conversations. She's a bird."

I didn't bring up that I had conversations with Crackers, and she wasn't the best conversationalist. I didn't think that would help me look any more normal. "Do you want to make any more animals?" I pointed to the pom-poms and pipe cleaners, hoping we could change the subject.

"What did you mean I might find out who you really are?" Katie asked. She didn't seem remotely interested in her three-headed dog anymore.

"I didn't mean anything by it. I don't even know why I said it."

Katie looked behind her to make sure the hallway was clear and then shut my door. She crouched down next to me and whispered in my ear. "Are there people listening to us?"

My eyes glanced over to the window to make sure my dad wasn't looking in. Katie saw me look at the window and her eyes widened. "Was someone spying through the window?" she whispered.

"No. How could anyone be spying on us? We're on the second floor," I pointed out.

Katie pointed to the glass box of pixie dust on my desk. "Is that a microphone?" She whispered so quietly I had to lean in to hear her.

"What? No. It's not a microphone." My eyes shot around the room looking for an option. "Do you want to do something else? We could play a board game or we could take Winston for a walk. "

"Yes! Let's take Winston for a walk," she said, talking superloud. "What a great idea!" Katie winked at me.

We tromped downstairs with Winston. Katie jumped a bit when she saw my parents waiting at the bottom of the stairs.

"Thank you so much for having me," Katie said. "Willow and I are going to take the dog for a walk. Not for any particular reason or anything. We don't need to be alone, we just feel like being outside." Katie was still talking in a really loud voice.

"Well, we're so glad you had a nice visit," my dad

said back, in a loud voice too. Maybe he thought Katie was hard of hearing. "You're welcome anytime!"

"Although be sure to call before you stop by," Mom said.

Lucinda didn't bother to come downstairs to say good-bye. She was most likely still hiding in her room.

Katie waited until we were down the block, with Winston walking ahead of us. She linked arms with me and leaned in to whisper in my ear again. "I don't think anyone can hear us out here. Now you can tell me."

"Tell you what?"

"Are you guys spies? Is your whole family in on it? Was the guest room full of computers and spy equipment, like cameras that can take pictures from space?" Katie kept shooting off questions. "I should have known. It explains so much. Are you spying on someone in this city? Are you hiding out from some evil government agency?"

Katie stopped, her mouth falling open. "Oh my gosh, can you fight like a ninja? If you wanted to, could you leap over that fence with, like, a single jump? They teach all kinds of cool stuff in spy school."

Winston snorted. "Are you going to tell her you can barely walk down the sidewalk without tripping over something? If you tried to leap over a fence like a ninja you would fall on your face."

"I'm not a spy," I explained to Katie. We started walking toward her house again.

"What about your dad?"

"He's not a spy either. Neither is my mom or sister." I felt bad telling her that. I could tell she had been excited about the idea of knowing a spy. If I thought I could pull it off, I would have let her believe I was a spy, but I figured sooner or later she would want to go on a spy mission with me, or expect me to make some kind of ninja jump, and then she would figure out the whole thing was a lie. Plus spies have all kinds of cool equipment like invisible ink pens, wire harnesses that let you hang off of a building a hundred stories up, or umbrellas that turn into swords. There was no way she would believe an orange that turned into a tiny coach was spy related.

"I figured your sister wasn't a spy. She's too high-strung," Katie said. "If she had to smuggle documents across the border, someone would guess she was up to something for sure."

"True," I admitted.

"So, if you aren't spies, then what are you?" Katie snapped her fingers. "I know, are you in the witness protection agency? Did your family testify in a trial of some famous criminal and now he's hunting you down?" Katie held her hand over her heart. "You can trust me. I would never tell on you guys. I can help. I can keep a lookout and make sure that no one sneaks up on you."

"We're not in the witness protection agency either." I kicked a loose stone on the sidewalk. It would be so much easier to tell her the truth, but I couldn't. It was against the rules. My parents would be so mad at me that I would be grounded until at least high school. Even worse than my parents, I didn't know what kind of trouble I would be in with the Fairy Council. Fairies had been in hiding from humans for hundreds of years. For all I knew, the administration might send me to jail. I liked Katie and I didn't want to lie to her, but I also didn't want to have to wear an orange jumpsuit for the rest of my life. I'd never see my family or Winston again. The idea of spending the rest of my life in a dungeon sounded like a very bad plan.

"Okay, be honest," Katie said. "Is your family actually

royalty from a really small country in Europe? If you're a princess, you can tell me. Maybe your family wants you to get to know ordinary people so you'll be a better ruler when the time comes. I've read about those kinds of things happening."

This is the problem with having a best friend who has a really good imagination and reads a lot. "No. I'm not a princess either. If I was a princess, would I have to clean my own room?" I pointed out.

"Maybe your parents want you to learn to clean so that you know how the rest of us live all the time," Katie suggested.

We stopped in front of Katie's house. "I'm positive I'm not a princess," I said.

"Then what is going on?" Katie held up her hand. "Don't even try and tell me that it's nothing. I'm not stupid. There's something happening at your house. Your parents and sister were acting all weird because I was over there and you had stuff you didn't want me to see. Best friends trust each other with their secrets," Katie pointed out.

I sighed. "You're going to have to trust me with this. I can't tell you what's going on. I can promise you that it isn't because I don't like you or think you're stupid.

You and I can still be best friends. We can still hang out together, but I can't tell you anything else."

Katie wouldn't look at me, but she didn't walk away either. I thought about trying to convince her, but I guessed this was one of those things she had to sort out on her own.

"Okay. I don't understand it, but if you can't tell me, I guess you can't."

"Still friends?" I asked softly.

"Of course." Katie threw her arm around me and gave me a hug. "Do you want to come over on Friday? It's pizza night. My mom lets you put whatever you want on your part of the pizza. Even peaches. The only thing is that you have to eat whatever you pick," Katie explained.

My heart sank. Choose-your-own-pizza-topping-night, and I had to miss it. My grandma had already arranged a meeting for me with the local area tooth fairy. There was no way I could reschedule *that*. If I didn't meet with her on Friday then Miranda would lose her tooth and the wedding could be ruined.

"I can't. I need to go to my grandma's that night," I explained.

Katie raised an eyebrow. "Can't you go another night?"

"It's sort of hard to explain, but, no, I can't."

"It's not hard to explain, you just won't explain it." Katie sighed, and I could tell she was still annoyed.

Wish-granting beats choose-your-own-pizza-topping-night, but unless you're willing to tell everyone you're a fairy godmother, there's no way to explain it.

sixteen

How long does it take to convince the Tooth Fairy to leave someone's tooth alone?

    a. Thirty minutes.

    b. Twenty-eight minutes, fifteen seconds.

    c. Who says you'll convince them at all?

Grandma set up a table and chairs in her garden. She said any warm days in late fall were to be enjoyed and shouldn't be squandered by spending time inside. She set the table with her fancy silver teapot and a plate of raspberry scones. Since she knew I didn't like tea, she made sure I had a glass of cold milk. Normally I preferred chocolate, but today I'd asked Grandma to make sure it was plain white milk. I pushed the glass to the center of the table.

"Hopefully, if she sees me drinking milk, she'll realize what good care I take of my own teeth. That might make her like me more." I reached into my pocket and pulled out a package of dental floss. "I flossed the past two days too."

Grandma patted my hand. "She'll find you charming."

"What if someone sees us out here?" I asked looking around the yard. I could just imagine how hard it would be to explain a tooth fairy to Grandma's neighbors. Her neighbor, Mr. Pollert, was always stopping by to bring Grandma some of his tomatoes or offering to mow her lawn. I think he liked her. Unlike fourth-grade boys, most grown up guys don't throw food at girls they like. However, just like fourth-grade boys, they don't seem able to just spit out what they think either.

"I'll make sure the gate is locked. No one will disturb you. You don't need to be nervous. All you have to do is tell her what you want and why it's so important."

There was a sharp rap on Grandma's front door at exactly 4:30. I stood up next to my chair while I waited for Grandma to lead her back into the garden. I'd changed after school into a skirt and sweater. It seemed like an important thing to try to look as grown up as possible. Part of being grown up seems to be wearing shoes that pinch your feet.

My mouth went dry when I saw Ms. McMillan walk out into the garden. She was wearing a gray pinstriped blazer with a gauzy pink skirt. She wore rhinestone cat's eye glasses. Her dark curly hair was pulled back into a bun that was so tight it made her eyes slant back. I had the feeling that her hair didn't dare disobey like mine did—always flopping one way or the other. Her skin was the color of chocolate milk and when she opened her mouth her teeth were blinding white.

Ms. McMillan looked at her arm. She had three watches on her wrist. "We have exactly thirty minutes for this discussion." She sat down and pulled out her briefcase. It was a hard enamel case in the shape of a molar with a gold chain shoulder strap. She clicked the molar open and pulled out a stack of folders.

I tried to swallow. My mind was completely blank. I couldn't think of what I had prepared to say. I noticed the pin on her lapel. It looked like a quarter; only it had diamonds around the edge.

"That's a pretty pin," I said.

She tapped the pin with one of her fingers. Her long

nails were painted a bright candy apple red. "I received this for having collected my one millionth tooth."

I tucked my hands under my skirt so she wouldn't see my ragged nails. "Wow. A million teeth seems like a lot."

"It is a lot. Do you know how someone gets to a million teeth?" She waited until I shook my head no before she continued. "They stay on schedule." She looked down at her watch. "Now we're down to twenty-eight minutes and fifteen seconds."

I swallowed and then jumped in. "I wanted to talk to you about a girl in my school, Miranda. She has a loose tooth and my grandma said she's supposed to lose it tonight."

The Tooth Fairy snapped her fingers and the teapot floated up in the air and poured a cup while she ran her fingernail down a spreadsheet. "Here she is, maxillary arch number eleven G." When she saw my face she clarified, "That means upper left canine tooth." She tapped on her tooth so I could see which one she was talking about. "Looks to me that she's been budgeted for five dollars." She pulled out her digital phone and checked something on the device. "It also appears this is her last baby tooth. Shame. Nice teeth. Some of the things I collect aren't worth a penny if you ask me. Your generation eats too much sugar."

I put down the cookie I was about to eat. "I was wondering if you might be willing to wait a day to take her tooth. She needs it for this wedding she's going to be in tomorrow," I explained.

"If I don't take her tooth then my register won't balance." She flipped the file so I could see the spreadsheet. There were columns and columns of names, what tooth, and the dollar figure. "I would be five dollars over."

"Is that a big deal?"

She raised an eyebrow and looked over the table at me. "I have a perfect record for balanced books. I've never been off as much as a dime." She pointed at me with the spreadsheet. "Not a single dime."

I shifted in my seat. "Maybe you could give me the five dollars today and then tomorrow after the wedding you could take Miranda's tooth. Then I could give her the five dollars."

"And I assume you have the magical ability to get the money under her pillow?"

I chewed on my lip. "Um. I could sneak it into her desk at school on Monday," I offered.

The Tooth Fairy shook her head. "I'm afraid that's not how this works. We're talking about thousands of years of tooth tradition. We can't have teeth staying when they're supposed to fall out, and money left in school desks or lunch bags. We have a system. We can't do things all higgledy-piggledy." She looked down at her watches to check the time and then finished her cup of tea.

"There has to be some sort of option," I pleaded before she could try to leave. "Just because we've always done things a certain way doesn't mean that's the way we should keep doing them. I've always thought putting the tooth under a pillow was a bit goofy. Wouldn't it make more sense to leave it by the toothbrushes in the bathroom?"

She looked at me in surprise. It didn't seem she had ever thought of this idea. She shook her head. "I think it's sweet you want to grant this humdrum's wish. I'm sure when you graduate from sprite school you'll make a great fairy godmother. However, I'm not comfortable with breaking the schedule." She started to push back from the table.

"Wait! You can't go!" I didn't know what to do. She was going to leave! Miranda would lose her tooth and

I would have totally bombed my very first wish-grant. My sister would never let me hear the end of it. I needed to keep her here until I could convince her to wait just one more day.

I whistled to the squirrels and raccoons that lived in Grandma's garden and begged for their help. They ran out from the trees and circled around Ms. McMillan, keeping her in place.

She held her molar briefcase close to her chest. "Good heavens. What are they doing?"

"I asked them to keep you here," I explained.

"You asked them?" She looked surprised.

"My special ability is magical communication. My sister can fly, but this comes in handy more often." I shrugged.

Ms. McMillan looked around the circle of animals. She put her hands on her hips. "You realize that you can't keep me against my will? You're standing in the way of official Tooth Fairy business." She pulled a note-book out of her molar bag. "All right. I want names."

The brown squirrel named Earnest shook his tail at her. "Do you want us to try and take her down?" He flexed his tiny biceps. "I've been working out."

Daisy, the chubby raccoon, twisted her paws

together. "Oh, I don't know about this. I'm already in trouble with my mom and dad for knocking over a bunch of trashcans."

"I don't want anyone to get in trouble, I just want to find a way to fix this problem. I'm sure there's a solution, we just have to think of it."

There was a loud rustle and then a crack. Then another problem fell from the tree with a short scream.

Katie.

seventeen

If your humdrum friend happens to spy on you and sees you talking to a tooth fairy, a bunch of squirrels, and a nervous raccoon, *and* doing magic, the way you could explain it would be:

a. ?!

b. ?!?!

c. ?!?!?!

d. I have no idea either.

Katie fell out of the tree and onto the ground with a loud *thunk*.

"Oh my gosh!" I ran over to Katie, but she was lying there with her eyes closed.

Earnest, the squirrel, scampered over and lifted her

eyelid with his tiny paw and peered in. "She's out. The fall must have knocked her out cold."

"Go get my grandma!" I yelled at Daisy. "Tell her there's been an accident." I crouched down next to Katie. I didn't know what to do so I waved my hands over her face to make sure she was getting enough air. If I were a couple years older I would have taken Sprite Emergency Training, but so far all I knew was that I shouldn't move her.

"Is that a humdrum girl?" Ms. McMillan looked down at Katie. "I think I know her. Does she live over on Pemberton Avenue? Nice molars, especially nineteen K, as I recall. What in the world was she doing in that tree?"

"She's my friend," I said. I swallowed a lump in my throat. I really hoped she was going to be okay. Katie must have followed me here. I should have known she would never settle for not knowing what was going on. Besides, after I lied about going to my grandma's last time to sneak off to Miranda's, it was no wonder she wanted to check out my story. She probably thought she was a modern day fourth-grade Sherlock Holmes.

"You know a humdrum personally?" the Tooth Fairy

asked, shocked. "I never heard of a fairy godmother of any level hanging out with a humdrum."

"She's not just a humdrum. Her name is Katie and she's my best friend," I said.

Katie's eyes fluttered open.

Grandma came running out of the backdoor with Daisy at her heels. "Let's get her inside." She said a quick spell, and Katie floated up off the ground and toward the house.

"Wow. I'm flying," Katie said, her voice all woozy.

"Technically you're floating, but there's no reason to quibble," Ms. McMillan pointed out. She followed us into the house, her high heels clicking on the stone tiles.

Grandma laid Katie out on the sofa and looked her over carefully. "There doesn't seem to be anything broken. Just a nasty bump on the head."

"No chipped teeth, that's good news," Ms. McMillan said, lifting up Katie's lip to look inside her mouth.

"Are you really the Tooth Fairy?" Katie asked. Before Ms. McMillan could even answer, Katie looked over at Grandma and me. "And you guys are fairies? That is so much cooler than being spies."

"Spies? What is she talking about? She must have hit her head pretty hard," Ms. McMillan said.

"It sort of makes sense if you know Katie," I explained. "She's not your average humdrum."

"What's a humdrum?" Katie asked, sitting up slowly. She was looking definitely much more alert and was peering around Grandma's living room with interest.

Grandma snapped her fingers and a plate of cookies floated into the room from the kitchen with a pitcher of milk. "This might take a while. We'll need a snack."

"I can't wait to hear how you're going to explain this," Ms. McMillan said, perching on the sofa.

"What about your oh-so-important schedule?" Grandma asked the Tooth Fairy.

"And miss this? Sometimes things are too interesting to stick to the schedule. It's been hundreds of years since a humdrum knew about the world of fairies. I'm not going to miss this, even for my schedule."

I seized the opportunity. "If you're willing to bend your schedule this one time, doesn't that mean that you could bend it again and take Miranda's tooth tomorrow instead of tonight?"

"The girl is trying to save a wedding, after all," Grandma pointed out.

Ms. McMillan threw up her hands. "Fine, this

Miranda girl can keep her tooth one extra day. I'll never hear the end of this from the Tooth Guild you know."

I almost jumped up and down I was so excited. The tooth was saved! The wedding was rescued! I looked down at Katie. It was all good news except for the part about my humdrum friend finding out about us being fairies. My parents and the Fairy Council might not be as impressed with my wish-granting abilities when they heard about this part of the story. "Is it too late to do a forget-me spell?" I asked Grandma.

"Forget-me spell? What's that?" Katie looked around waiting for something exciting to happen.

"A forget-me spell puts a person's memories in rewind. For you it would seem like déjà vu. You would be outside the gate again, thinking it felt like you had been there before, but you wouldn't remember anything after that. Not the tree, or what you heard or right now. We fairies use it when a humdrum, that's a human like yourself, accidentally sees some magic they weren't supposed to," Grandma explained.

"But I don't want to forget this! This is the best thing ever!" Katie said.

"You don't need to worry. Too much time has passed.

There is only so much memory that is safe to rewind, and we have to do it instantly. If we try and erase too much, the person can end up with amnesia. The last thing we want is you wandering around not knowing even your own name. I think we have no choice but to trust you with the truth," Grandma said.

"Oh boy, am I in trouble when my parents hear about this." I grabbed a couple extra cookies off the platter. I might as well enjoy myself now. Once my parents found out that I was the one responsible for breaking thousands of years of hiding from humdrums I was going to wish my life was over. This was way worse than the one time I tried to swat my sister with a magazine when she was flying.

"Lean back, Katie, this is a long story," Grandma said.

"A long time ago in a world far, far away, fairies and humans used to live in harmony . . ."

Katie didn't say a word the entire time Grandma told her about fairy history, with certain fairies playing tricks on humans, humans deciding to lock up fairies, and fairies going into hiding. She was so interested in the story she didn't even have any cookies. I had three. I might have eaten four except the Tooth Fairy pointed to the cookies and then to my teeth, reminding me that maybe I'd already had enough sugar.

"So no one knows you exist?" Katie whispered.

"No. As far as any humdrums know, we are humans just like them," Grandma said.

"I always sort of wondered if there might really be fairies," Katie said. "It seemed to me that the world would be a better place with magic."

"Oh, it is." Grandma nodded her agreement.

"But why are fairies becoming less magical?" Katie asked, concerned.

"No one is sure, but some of us are working on some theories," Grandma said. "However, we're going to have to ask you to keep this a secret. I'm not sure the rest of the humdrum world would be quite so happy to find out that magic and fairies are real."

"I promise." Katie held up her right hand like she was taking an oath. She fidgeted on the sofa. "Can I see you do some more magic?"

"Not today, we should get you home. It's getting late. Next time Willow is over you'll have to have her talk to your pet bird for you," Grandma said.

"You can understand animals?! Is that why you were talking to Winston the other day at your house? You can hear what he's thinking?" Katie looked at me, impressed.

I blushed. "It's sort of a rare magical talent. Not every fairy godmother can do it."

Grandma got up and wrapped up a plate of cookies and handed them to Katie. "Here, you can take these home with you."

"This has been the most awesome day ever," Katie said. "This is better than being shot into space."

"That's high praise, coming from you," Grandma said.

Katie hugged me and then went to the front door. "You can count on me. I'll never tell a soul."

I waved as she ran out the door. I knew I had picked the best humdrum in the whole world to be my best friend. She thought magic was cool *and* she could keep a secret. If I had picked someone like Bethany to be my best friend then she would have already blabbed to the TV news stations.

"Willow, don't tell your parents about all this until I've had a chance to sort this out," Grandma said. "I need to think of the best way to tell this news to the Fairy Council so that we don't have a panic on our hands."

"This certainly was an interesting afternoon: humdrums falling out of trees, changing tooth schedules, coming out of hiding. I hope we don't have to disappear again." Ms. McMillan said. "That will really mess up my schedules."

"She promised not to tell," I reminded everyone. "No one has to hide from Katie and no other humdrums need to know."

"She might be your best friend, but there's no guarantee the Fairy Council is going to believe she'll keep our secret. They may want all of us to disappear again. It's just a shame the girl saw us," Ms. McMillan said. She looked down at her watches. "I should go. I might be giving Miranda's tooth a pass tonight, but the rest of them aren't going to collect themselves."

My eyebrows crunched up together. How had Katie gotten into the backyard? "I thought you had locked the back garden gate?" I asked Grandma.

Grandma looked away. "I must have forgotten. I meant to lock it."

Ms. McMillan gathered up her molar briefcase, shoving all of her spreadsheets inside. "It's almost enough to make someone believe that you wanted a humdrum to find us."

"Don't be silly, of course I didn't plan for this to happen," Grandmother said. "We'll just have to take this one step at a time and see what happens next."

eighteen

True or False:

You never know what will happen when you are with your best friend.

Answer:

Absolutely True.

I jumped out of bed on Saturday morning and rushed to look out the window. The sun was shining. It was a perfect day for a wedding. I suspected that might have been something my mom had done because it was supposed to rain.

The doorbell rang right after lunch. Lucinda opened the door and screamed. My parents and I ran to see what happened. Lucinda had already slammed the door shut and was on her tiptoes looking through the peephole.

"It's that humdrum, Katie," Lucinda said. "I opened the door and there was a humdrum *right there*. I wasn't aware that because we had her over once that she was going to be coming by all the time. I think I should get a warning if there are going to be humdrums popping up all the time."

"It's not all the time and you can't slam the door on her, that's rude." I stepped past Lucinda and opened the door. I really hoped Katie remembered to keep everything a secret the way Grandma asked her. "Hi, Katie. It sure is a nice ordinary day out isn't it?"

Katie noticed my parents and Lucinda standing right behind me. "Yes, it sure is. Nothing out of the ordinary at all." We both smiled at my parents to show just how normal everything was. "I wondered if you might want to come over and play," Katie said. "You could bring Winston if he wanted to come. I mean, not that you would know if he wanted to come, because it isn't like you could understand him, but if you thought he might like it then he would be welcome."

"I'd love to come, but I promised to go with my mom to deliver a wedding cake," I explained. "Miranda's cousin is getting married today."

Katie's face fell. "Oh."

"Maybe you could come with us." I turned to look at Mom.

"Oh, I don't know . . . ," Mom stammered.

"I'm not real crazy about weddings," Katie said. I knew she also meant she wasn't real crazy about Miranda, but she was too nice to say it.

"It'll be fun, and it won't take too long to drop off the cake," I said. I could tell Katie really wanted to hang out more than she minded going to the wedding. She nodded.

"All right. You girls go ahead and jump into the van. We need to get that cake to the reception hall."

My mom's bakery van was glossy white with a giant pink cupcake on the side. "Enchanted Sugar" was in glittery blue letters on the door. The van always looked perfect because my mom had done a spell so mud never stuck to the side.

The wedding reception was being held in a fancy hotel downtown. The hotel manager showed us the room. There were white lights strung through potted trees all along the walls and each table was covered in thick, cream-colored tablecloths with giant floral arrangements in the center. Crystal chandeliers sparkled in the candlelight.

"Wow. It looks like a fairy tale!" Katie said when we walked into the room. She then slapped her hand over her mouth. "I mean, it looks like a castle."

Mom looked at Katie with one eyebrow raised. Before she could ask anything, I cut her off. "I bet the guests will be here soon," I said. "We better hurry to get the cake set up."

We pushed the cake trolley to the display table and the waiters helped my mom move the cake over. It looked perfect. Mom bustled around making last minute touch-ups to the icing. Katie and I helped by tucking tiny pink rosebuds all around the bottom of the cake plate. When Katie turned to get more flowers Mom blew a pinch of pixie dust over the cake to help ensure a happy-ever-after.

There was a bustle out in the hallway and then wedding guests started to pour into the room.

"We should go," Mom said brushing her hands off. "I have to go back to the bakery to sign for a delivery."

"Can Katie and I stay for a bit so we can see the bride? We can walk home from here," I asked. I could tell my mom was about to say no. "Please! This is our first wedding."

"All right, but remember, we're not guests. Don't stay too long. Call me when you get home." Mom rolled the cake trolley out of the room.

"I know you don't want to stay, but we won't be long. I just want to see everyone. Besides, we can get ice cream on the way home, my treat," I offered. Katie sighed. We were standing near the back, when I saw the first pink bridesmaid enter the room. "Here they come!"

"If I could get the wedding party all over here by the cake," the photographer called out. He arranged the wedding party in a half circle around the table. Miranda looked great and you couldn't tell at all that birds had gone crazy with her dress.

"Hey, isn't that the Tooth Fairy?" Katie elbowed me and pointed out to the hallway.

I followed her finger and saw Ms. McMillan standing in the hall. She was leaning against the wall pretending to talk on her phone.

"Last picture everyone! Big smiles!" the photographer called out. The camera flashed.

Ms. McMillan nodded at Katie and me and then tapped her front tooth.

I spun around. Miranda's eyes were wide and she closed her mouth with a snap. She tugged on the sleeve of her mom's dress and I saw her reach into her mouth and pull out her tooth. She and her mom hustled off to the bathroom.

Ms. McMillan snapped her phone shut and gave us a small salute before she disappeared into the crowd.

"She didn't wait a second longer than she had to, did she?" Katie asked.

"Tooth fairies are like that. A bit schedule driven." My mouth was in a thin line. I hoped the missing tooth wouldn't bother Miranda too much. All the formal pictures of the wedding party were done.

Katie nudged me. "Don't be sad. Everything turned out perfectly!"

I smiled. "You're right. It did." My first wish-grant wasn't the easiest thing I'd ever done, but for my first time it hadn't gone too badly.

Katie suddenly yanked on my arm. "You're floating!" She hissed.

I looked down, shocked. My feet were about a six inches off the floor. Holy cow. "This isn't possible," I said.

Katie let go of my arm and I started to go higher. She

grabbed me again and pulled me back down. "Cut it out or people are going to see."

"I'm not doing it on purpose. I'm not supposed to float."

"Maybe you're not supposed to, but you are," Katie said, pointing out the obvious.

"But you don't understand, each fairy godmother gets one special power, everything else is a learned spell. I already have my one power." My mind raced, trying to make sense of what was happening. "I have to talk to my grandma about this right away."

"The first thing we need to do is figure out how to get you out of here without anyone noticing. I can't exactly leave leading you out of here like a balloon. Can you get down?"

"I'm not sure how this works. I've never floated before. I'll try." I closed my eyes and pictured myself down on the ground. "Is it working?" I whispered to Katie.

"You sort of bopped around a bit, but you're still a few inches above the ground." Katie looked around the room. She was starting to sweat. She wasn't used to magic going wrong like I was. If she thought this was stressful, she was lucky she hadn't been around the time I set a bunch of pixies free in the grocery store by accident.

"Okay, you're going to have to call Grandma. Don't worry, she'll know what to do. I'll hang on to this tree until you get back." I gripped the trunk of the potted ficus tree and held myself as close to the ground as possible.

"Are you sure?" Katie asked.

"We can't wait here until I float up to the ceiling. Someone's bound to notice sooner or later." I quickly told her Grandma's humdrum phone number. Katie dashed out of the reception hall and into the lobby where there was a phone. I tried to look casual bopping my head to the music. My arm was getting sore from holding myself down. If this was going to happen more often I was going to need to do more chin-ups in gym class and build up my biceps.

After a few minutes Katie came back, weaving her way through the wedding guests. "Your grandma is on her way. She's superexcited. She thinks the fact you're floating proves her theory."

"What theory?"

"Because I believe in you, your powers are stronger," Katie said. "Fairies' power is connected to having people believe in the magic."

"Then I guess I'm pretty lucky you're my best friend," I said.

Katie smiled. "Yeah, you are pretty lucky."

I giggled and went to punch her in the arm. When I let go of the tree I started to float up again which made us giggle louder. Katie grabbed me before I could get too high.

Katie suddenly stopped giggling. "Uh-oh. Miranda's seen us. She's coming over here."

I turned and noticed was Miranda walking toward us. "If she gets too close she's going to see I'm not touching the ground." I looked at the door, hoping that my grandma would appear.

"Think heavy thoughts," Katie said. "Like cement, wet laundry . . ."

"Rocks, my Aunt Haddie's scones . . . ," I said, noting that I was starting to sink the last few inches toward the floor.

"Cannonballs, stacks of library books, your mom's van." Katie kept listing off every heavy thing that came into her mind. My feet touched the floor and stayed there just in time.

"Hi, Miranda," I said.

"Your mom's cake turned out perfect!" Miranda gushed. "Everyone says it's the prettiest wedding cake they've ever seen."

"Thanks. You look really nice," I said.

Miranda laughed and spun in a circle so her dress would flare out. "You should stay! There's lots of food and there's going to be dancing later. My cousin would love for you to be here, since your mom made the cake." She looked at Katie as if she just noticed her there. "I'd invite you too, Katie, but I'm not sure it would be okay. I'm sure you understand."

Katie's shoulders dropped. She started to take a step back.

I linked arms with Katie to keep her right next to me. "Thanks for the invitation, Miranda, but Katie and I have plans for the rest of the day."

Miranda was shocked. "You're not going to stay? Anyone at school would give anything to be here."

"Not me. I'd give anything to spend the day with my best friend. Tell your cousin I said congratulations."

Katie and I walked out of the reception arm in arm. Going to the wedding would be fun, but not nearly as much fun as spending the day with my best friend. Weddings are pretty cool, but a good best friend can keep your feet on the ground.

nineteen

Having a humdrum best friend who knows you are a fairy and believes in you means:

a. that you'll develop new magical skills, like floating, which will drive your sister crazy because she only has one magical power.

b. if you do start to float, you can count on her to come up with an idea to keep you from floating away.

c. you'll have to translate what her annoying pet bird wants all the time because her bird always has something to say.

d. no one is exactly sure what it means, but I bet it will be an adventure!

Definitely, this is an "all of the above" kind of situation.

Find out what happens next in

Fourth Grade Fairy #3:
Gnome Invasion

one

Being able to shrink down and fly:
  a. is way more fun than you might have thought it
      would be.
  b. really ticks off your know-it-all older sister
      because she thought it was her special ability.
  c. comes in handy, especially if you want to spy on
      your sister.
  d. all of the above.

Katie flopped across my bed, nearly landing on my dog Winston who had been sleeping under the covers. "I want to visit the Fairy Academy if there are boys who look like that!"

"You should see Evan play draolo. He's amazing," I said.

"What's that?" Katie asked, sitting up and scratching Winston's ears.

"Draolo. It's like polo only with dragons." Katie's eyes grew wide, so I went on to explain so she wouldn't have the wrong idea. "They're not huge dragons or anything. They're raised for the game, sort of horse-size, but they can snort fire and fly."

"That is so cool. I would love to own a pet dragon," Katie said.

Winston rolled over so Katie could rub his belly. "Pfft, why would anyone want a dragon as a pet when they could have a dog?" he asked. "Dogs are superior creatures in almost every way."

Since I was the one who could communicate with animals I had to translate for Katie. "Winston thinks you're better off with a dog. He's a bit of a dog snob, but he is right about this. Dragons are okay, but they aren't housebroken and they can be kind of smelly," I warned Katie.

"Still, it's a dragon. I bet Evan looks really cute riding one." Katie sighed, and then perked up. "Maybe we should make up a plate of your mom's cookies and bring them to Evan and your sister. Doing homework can make someone pretty hungry. Giving people food isn't bugging them, it's being polite."

"It is polite, but my sister will freak out and say we're doing it just to spy on her," I explained. Katie looked annoyed. I had tried to tell her before how lucky she was to be an only child. Now she was starting to understand what a pain older sisters could be.

"Do you think Evan likes your sister?"

I scrunched up my eyebrows while I thought about it. It was possible. I wasn't exactly an expert on boys. Everyone kept telling me that Nathan Filler in my class liked me because he would tease me and throw the fries from his hot lunch at me. It didn't make sense to me, but humdrum boys are complicated. My sister, despite her many flaws, was pretty. Plus, she tended to keep her really evil behavior directed at me. She was usually quite nice to other people. "He might like her. He wouldn't have to help with her potion homework. He must be doing it for a reason."

"I wonder what they're talking about?" Katie asked.

"I bet they're talking about us," I said. "It's a really big deal to other fairies that we're friends."

"Don't you want to know what he thinks? We could

send Winston down to listen to their conversation and then come back and tell us what he said," Katie suggested.

"I beg your pardon! I have no intention of getting involved in some sort of boy-crazy spy mission." Winston rolled over so he could stand.

"We could give him some bologna to make it worth his time." Katie might not be able to understand Winston the same way that I did, but she was a pretty good at knowing what made him tick.

Winston's head cocked over to the side. "Bologna? Now, maybe I was being a bit hasty when I said I wouldn't do it. I would consider simply strolling downstairs, and if I happened to overhear a discussion, there certainly isn't anything sneaky about sharing the details." Winston's tongue fell out of his mouth as he started thinking about a giant mound of bologna slices.

"Easy, my canine James Bond." I turned to Katie. "This plan won't work. Lucinda knows I can communicate with Winston. No way she would let him wander into the room, plop down, and listen. She'd kick him out of the living room so fast all we would see would be a furry black blur."

The three of us were silent while we tried to think of a plan that would work.

"You could still get me some bologna. I think better with processed meat snacks." Winston turned in a circle to mat the bedspread into a comfy pile and then flopped down with his head on his paws.

"What I wouldn't give to be a fly on the wall," Katie said.

Katie and I both looked over at each other at the same second and squealed. It was a perfect plan.

Eileen Cook spent most of her teen years wishing she was someone else or somewhere else, which is great training for a writer. When she was unable to find any job postings for world famous author positions, she went to Michigan State University and became a counselor so she could at least support her book-buying habit. But real people have real problems, so she returned to writing. She liked having the ability to control the ending, which is much harder to do when you're a human.

Eileen lives in Vancouver with her husband and dogs and no longer wishes to be anyone or anywhere else. You can read more about Eileen, her books, and the things that strike her as funny at eileencook.com.